AF265287

MEMENTO POSTRIDIE

by

Trevor P. Kwain

Published by Threepeppers Publishing
Translated in English by Carol Winteringham

2nd Edition – January 2016
First published in Italian in Great Britain in 2013

ISBN: 978-0-9574113-6-4

Cover:
The sad shadow of the Duomo of Milan
Drawing © 2016 Trevor P. Kwain

www.3peppers.co.uk

www.trevorpkwain.org

To Aldous Huxley and my Grandfather

Foreword

The theme of Memento Postridie is not about scientific progress in itself; it is more about how progress of science has influenced human individuals.

"The triumphs of physics, chemistry and engineering are implicitly taken for granted. It is only by means of biological sciences that quality of life can radically change. The other scientific fields may be applied in such a way as to destroy life or make it extremely complex and difficult. The real revolution is to be found not in the external world but within the body and soul of man. [...] With this book I have chosen to summarise numerous future predictions; not for the mere pleasure of foreseeing but also to understand how our lives and habits could suddenly change. Science will not stop and if it continues at this pace, what we can see today might not exist in the future."

Aldous Huxley

I wrote *Memento Postridie* back in 2000, at the dawn of the 21st century, and still today it amazes me of how I could have imagined the future described in the story. When I finally managed to publish the book for the first time in 2012, many things had changed, including myself. I felt the urge to make changes or corrections since some things I predicted years ago came true somehow but maybe not as accurately as portrayed in the book. However, it would have been a big mistake to do so, a botched up job. I hope you enjoy it.

Trevor P. Kwain

I

Deep into the night, darkness reigned everywhere both inside and outside the apartment blocks. If you listened carefully you could still faintly hear the dull whistle of the Darkening in the distance, although the alarm had actually gone off about three hours before and now the streets were without any kind of lighting, leaving a kind of stillness. Only the moon peeped out from behind the clouds in the cold autumnal sky. It seemed to be the only living thing in these peaceful residential districts of Milan. Everyone was sound asleep in their beds except for one person who just could not live with his thoughts in that deathly silence.

The mechanical wind up clock in Room 221b had just struck eleven p.m. and for the umpteenth time Andrea Rossi had got ready for bed knowing it would be another sleepless night. Obviously his room too was in absolute darkness and all the furniture had lost its concreteness, becoming shadowy silhouettes. Andrea's only source of light came from a small candle which he kept in a drawer and took out in moments like this one, when the power was momentarily suspended. Everything else had to be turned off after the Darkening even the liquid crystal clock with its cheerful buzz. All this created a kind of stillness offering no sign of the passing of time. Of course Andrea was used to this by now so he just sat at his desk in the living room for about half an hour without taking much notice of anything. He usually sat staring at the white walls in front of him but he also frequently sat with his head lowered looking down at the white empty pages of a diary. The hands of the windup clock showed eleven ten now but Andrea had not noticed. He pulled out the drawer, took out the famous diary without making the slightest noise. It had a velvety, worn out red cover; it must have been at least ten years old although the pages and binding seemed new. Andrea went straight to the first page and took pen in hand. No sooner had he picked it up that a strange feeling, a feeling of clumsiness came over him as it were the first time he had ever used such a tool. He could not even start to imagine how people once upon a time would write with such old tools and how lucky he was that now everything was written and printed via a fifteen inch screen. Pens and pencils were things of the past. Andrea would have rather used digital technology but computer writing at his hour of the day was impossible; so he took to diary and pen. Unfortunately, the task was harder than he had imagined, his hand already ached, having to hold the pen in a fixed way and he was sure that after writing for a few minutes, his fingers would be numb. Andrea was determined however, so he started to write:

Letter I – Milan 6th November 2073

Andrea stopped writing, not out of pain but just to read through what he had written: writing was so simple but felt so strange. He glanced at the date and suddenly his thoughts became lost in a cloudy confusion of images and words. Working in an office meant many dates had come and gone but he had never really considered the idea of how this simple number indicated the passing of time. It had never crossed his mind because every day seemed alike, just like every year and like all his life. Just recently he kept on having strange thoughts which led him to useless meditation and reflections and it was this that would not let him sleep. At first he put it down to tiredness but as it got worse it started to have negative effects on his work. The Firm advised him to get a check-up with their team of doctors but had been a waste of time. Useless because it was not a simple headache or even a trauma but something which lay much deeper, coming from his inner soul. Even now Andrea did not fully understand what was wrong with him, despite his sensations, except that everything seemed to be taking on a new meaning which he could not yet grasp.

Andrea went back to his writing trying to change subject but every time he saw the diary he could not help going back to some of his old thoughts. Why had he opened this diary? This was a difficult question but he felt he had to get something off his chest. He knew he had to get the long monologue that had been going round and round in his head for days, down onto the empty pages. He took up his pen, eyes closed, and let his mind lead his hand.

No-one stops to think anymore.

Andrea rubbed his eyes. The words had flowed out so easily just like water flowing over a smooth stone. The result was amazing. He had already heard this sentence somewhere before maybe about a week ago.

That day Andrea had left work two hours earlier and it was a real relief to finish before time. When he usually wanted to leave early the CEO would ask him if he could manage some overtime, but that day no request came and he was out of the office by five. It was too early to go back home so Andrea decided to go around the centre for a while making use of the unreserved *transport*. The few times Andrea had managed to get some time off he had never found any *transport* – it was all reserved. This did not mean he could not go into the town centre to enjoy the shops but without *transport* both his office and his apartment were quite a way from Piazza Duomo. Sometimes the reservations could last days or even weeks but everyone had got used to it, knowing that it would end sooner or later. In the last thirty years the petrol crisis had hit the whole world and at first just the thought of having to limit the use of electricity and respect the Darkening seemed almost impossible, but in time everyone had come to accept it. Andrea just like everybody else saw the crisis as a part of their routine so there was no sign of panic and never had been. So life carried on, technology progressed and energy continued to be used in a limited way without creating too many problems. Occasionally the President of Global Corp. communicated the assets of the moment. They were a series of decreasing numbers whose order was not always entirely clear to the multitudes who passed in front of the *dvd-screen* or even stopped to see a multimedia copy of Time. The announcement lasted just a few minutes, enough time to announce any important data while everyone stood waiting holding their breaths and then ahhhh! the tension vanished without leaving a trace and everyone went back to what they had been doing a few moments before. How could the crisis be a risk if people were still enjoying all the advantages of modern technology? Andrea reasoned in the same way too, not caring about the situation and every day he would turn on the lights, his microwave, computer and CD player.

There were only a few people in town and nobody was standing at the bus stop. His *transport* came half empty and came bluntly to a halt. He got on and sat on one of the front seats without looking to see if anyone else was on board although the irritating laughs of a group of youths sitting at the back of the bus could not go unheard. It was not that Andrea hated young people but they reminded him of his youth, a series of unconnected and not so happy events. Along the way from Piazza Firenze to Piazza Della Scala he tried not to listen to the noise the boys were making but as he got lost in his thoughts he could not help remembering. His childhood had not been the greatest; he had spent most of his early years in a children's home surrounded by women in white coats and other orphaned children. He had never known who his mother was; maybe she had left him on the roadside when he was a mere new born. He had never had a dad as his mum has decided to opt for artificial insemination. Andrea felt no resent for a mother who he had no recollection of, but he could not bear the fact that he had been abandoned after she had decided to opt for a test tube baby. That was the way of the world and you ended up going along with the masses without worrying too much about the fact that perhaps you in the future could do the same harm to someone and they would suffer just like you. Andrea had been to the Sperm Bank several times to curse them and his colleague who had convinced him to donate his sperm into a plastic tube. Unfortunately there was no turning back so it was best forgotten.

The *transport* continued on its way then the driver rang his bell and braked suddenly which made Andrea jump and bring him back to reality. The group of youths had already got off and although he had not seen their faces, he saw their baggy jeans and grey velvet jackets and shaved heads as they went off into the distance. Andrea looked out of the misty window and noticed the time on the clock; it was five fifteen. It was well and truly dark now and the *transport* lights were switched on just as the yellow street lights came on spreading a feeble light over the roads. Andrea got off calmly turning up his collar against the cold breeze. On the road people wrapped up in their coats were making their way to the Galleria Vittorio Emanuele or the bus stops or to where Andrea was going.

Piazza Duomo was just as beautiful as ever, even more so, since they had put up laser lighting on the pinnacles of the Cathedral. What a wonderful sight! They were the only lights to remain on after the Darkening came and spread their light through the dark, impenetrable sky out over the city. They could be admired at their best at night from the higher floors of the apartments and they had become the only attraction after the Darkening. The chance to gaze at these four lights shining to the right then to the left was not really that exciting but on those solitary nights they were a kind of comfort. Andrea thought they were a waste of money and of no help whatsoever for his sleeplessness, but at the same time he could not help but admire them and admit they were beautiful and majestic. It was his own attitude that annoyed him most: it was one of those irritating symptoms that had been continually affecting him. His opinions always contradicted themselves: there was a big difference in what he liked outside and what he liked on the inside so he felt on edge whenever he spoke to someone and for a short time he decided not to talk a lot to people, to avoid conversations with friends and colleagues in order to hide his ill being. When he was on his own however, his inner thoughts made him feel worse. The only way out was to stop playing the psychologist and get on with life.

Andrea strolled toward the end of the Galleria. On the right hand corner near one of the smog blackened columns a band of musicians were playing and singing *technoplus* music. The loud bass guitar pounded out the rhythm with the drums accompanied by electronic vibrations which pumped out an even beat. This kind of music did not appeal to Andrea but it was popular with young and old alike at the moment. A large crowd had gathered to listen, some were jumping to the sound while others were going wild. They looked like street players but in fact they were the live band providing entertainment for the nearby eating house. It was an extension of the *iperco-op* McDonald-Nestlé where the best grilled paninis could be devoured. It was not the only eating place, there were a lot more spread over the fifteen floors of this enormous building, five square kilometres wide and so high that it almost touched the sky. Someone had said that the *iperco-ops* were much taller in the USA reaching even forty floors in height. These immense *iperco-ops* had everything. There were four which faced onto Piazza Duomo and they lit up the whole square with their multi-coloured lights. Sweet sounds and melodies echoed everywhere trying to induce people to buy. At least two hundred megaphones filled the air announcing the latest offers and discounts in joyful tones. Lights and sounds stimulated the eyes and ears of the Milanese people. According to Global Corp. they were the only buildings that could have two extra hours of electric lighting. The *iperco-ops* stayed open until ten p.m. while the rest of the city was already in darkness. This privilege was due to the fact that you could find absolutely everything in these mega stores; there was no need to search elsewhere. They were so colourful decorated with umpteen "Ms" and red logos. They were a praise to opulence, a symbol of wealth and well-being. The shelves had every kind of dish from simple vegetables to frozen foods, meat to tinned goods, everything man could wish for was replenished daily, twenty hour seven, three hundred days of the year. If you did not have time to cook, you could choose to eat at one of the many eating houses open nonstop and choose any kind of cuisine from Indian Madras curry to Mexican tacos or Japanese Teppan-yaki or Spaghetti alla Bolognese. Everything was available and nutritious: it was all genetically modified. Food was created in the bio-agriculture establishments on the Padana Plain. The *pharmafarmers* had the task of extracting the DNA from plants and animals to make them resistant to any kind of disease or intemperate climate while the *ecoscouts* had the task of checking the safety of the production area to prevent any bad surprises coming from the ecosystem. The genetically modified plants were then ready to be put into green houses that had been built onto the establishments. Andrea had never actually seen these establishments but he had come to learn about them from his online *ekletto-encyclopaedia*. He has seen photos and various statistics about them. He knew they were in the country, in far off deserted places that were never easy to reach. He did not care so much about it as only staff were allowed to go inside. It would be a waste of time to go there.

Opposite the *iperco-op* McDonald-Nestlé was another mega store, the Laurent-Chanel, which dealt exclusively in clothes. It covered the other half of the Galleria for another two square kilometres toward Piazza Babila and the Public Gardens. The most interesting part of the Lauren-Chanel building was its exterior. It was an extravagant building with weird decorations and statues lit up on each façade with psychedelic lights. It was even more creative inside: asymmetric aisles, off shooting staircases, extra-white walls and minimalist furniture but with such detail that gave it a wonderful touch of class. On each of the fifteen floors, garments of every description were on display from tail coat jackets to tuxedos, from beat generation clothes to rave, from beachwear to sportswear in every style imaginable with every kind of mix and match, in all the fifty-seven thousand six hundred different shades.

The strong lights of the Laurent-Chanel store were slightly obfuscated by the third *iperco-op* in front of it which made use of the latest brilliant digital technology. The New Microsoft-Sony was an expert in its field: each electronic gadget had its own specific sector from the small electrical appliances to stereos, from new generation computers to satellite TVs. This store was the tallest; it had twenty floors and spread as far as Piazza Medaglia d' Oro. It was divided into two parts: one opened up onto Piazza Duomo as this was the technology outlet, while the other was more of a warehouse to stock goods coming in. There was a transporter tunnel from the eighth floor which led to the station of Porta Romana. The goods were sent from here to or away from Milan. It was a brilliant system enabling goods to be moved quickly and easily. It guaranteed a safe transport system thanks to the use of advanced robots. Automation had reached maximum level now so manual labour was no longer required. The New Microsoft-Sony had been a leader company in the past and so now it had become the symbol of progress. Consequently it was the most popular store and every day millions of people passed through their aisles even if it was just to buy some batteries or a virgin mini disc. The large crowds were also due to the fact that the Policlinic Hospital sat in the in the middle of the New Microsoft–Sony building. A lot of their customers were indeed surgeons and *v-dentists*, tissue engineers, genetic programmers and nurses. The hospital linked up with the fourth *iperco-op* which was also just as popular. It was the Amazon-Virgin store which sold a wide variety of objects and accessories as well as housing the CRS and the GASDAQ. It went as far as Via De Amicis and closed up the commercial circle.

All of these four *iperco-ops* formed the large world company known as Global Corp. that had decided fifty years ago to get rid of every tiny shop on the corner of every street and abolish every small business and unify them finally under one name. In this way with the help of the World Wide Web the market had become one capable of reaching every corner of the earth without obstacles or barriers. The system had been weak at first but slowly globalization brought about a swift and perfect production system. Many years had passed since this great economic revolution had changed the future of the world and now world populations enjoyed a good quality of life by being able to find anything they needed in one of the *iperco-ops* without looking elsewhere. This major event had been described in every online library, every *ekletto-*

encylopedia and over time it had become an important event in the history of mankind but just like any historical fact this too had simply turned into yet another mental notion which was kept alive only by those who were aware of it. Andrea was one of those types because he enjoyed reading a lot. He certainly was not an idiot and detested to be considered one by some people.

The square was crowded just like it always is, with people coming and going in all directions. Everyone was busy going about their daily chores- shopping or whatever and occasionally you could come across an old friend amid the crowd in that one area of the city where everyone came together. Andrea stepped out from out of the arches and looked up toward the sky. It was a full moon and it shone brightly despite the various bright lights. On the top floor of the McDonald-Nestlé building you could just see the soft light blue lights of the Blue Moon terrace, the most chic restaurant in all Milan. Andrea gazed at the silence up high and looked down at the chaos below: he decided to turn left toward the Lauren-Chanel building so as not to bump into someone he did not really want to see. He strolled passed the shop windows with his head slightly turned down and his collar turned up to keep warm. He occasionally lifted his head to glance at the people coming toward him or to see if there were any synthetic deer skin jackets but he did not see the man coming up from behind.

'Mr. Rossi!' exclaimed the man.

Andrea spun round and saw a pair of fine glasses and a nice red nose. It was Gianni Vazzano, the Firm's psychologist that Andrea had been forced to see for the last two weeks. He had bumped into the last person he wanted to see, after all his efforts.

'Hello there Mr. Vazzano, you look well.' replied Andrea, smiling and trying to seem surprised.

'I wouldn't say well!' replied the psychologist. 'I've had this awful cold for the last five days and it won't leave me in peace. Look at my nose!'

Andrea changed his smile without revealing his irritation. Of course he could see his red nose, that large thing right in front of him and the more Andrea stepped back the more Vazzano moved closer. This wasn't the first time it had happened, he would do the same when Andrea was on the psychologist's couch and he could smell his bad breath. Here in the open air and more space it was different but Andrea was still on edge at Vazzano's presence. How could he bluntly tell him his nose was disgusting and he was really horrible? What right did he have? Andrea felt a kind of click in his head and without thinking answered in a casual tone.

'Don't worry about it. Have you thought of going to see a skin engineer?'

'I'm not sure. I had thought of taking a stabilizer. Thanks for the advice anyway. When's your next sitting?'

Andrea didn't want to be analysed by someone like Vazzano anymore. He wanted to say 'No', a decisive 'No' but then he thought that maybe the Firm was right.

'Thursday' Andrea said in a half cordial, half irritated tone. Andrea was really cross with himself. Why hadn't he been able to say what he was thinking instead of conforming to other people's words or those of the Firm? Suddenly Andrea felt another click in his head. Vazzano went on talking but Andrea was no longer listening.

'Right then, Mr. Rossi, see you Thursday. I'm in a bit of a rush and I need to be home before the Darkening. I still haven't found a suit. I was looking for a classical suit but there were so many that I didn't buy anything. In half an hour I have to attend the online in advanced psycho-analysis as well as getting a bite to eat – a Pizza Big American. I might have time tonight to read something on my new portable Opsolector, one of the few gadgets which still go on batteries. Damn it, I won't make it. It's almost impossible to keep to one's schedule. But we must try. Bye!'

A third click went off in Andrea's head. He was perplexed. Difficult to explain how he felt but he did realize how it made him feel more and more uneasy. He said a straight goodbye to Vazzano who disappeared without seeing Andrea's vacant look. Andrea stepped aside away from the crowd. He leant against the wall and put his hand to his head .He stared down at the dark, dirty paving, the piles of dirty black litter pushed up against the wall and the recently dropped cigarette ends. The ash was still alight and Andrea watched the cigarette ends die out, how the paper quickly curled up. It was a simple chemical process but Andrea observed it just the same. He watched the smoke floating up here and there without rising vertically. He recognised the brand name as it burnt up and disappeared in a veil of greyish dust. When the cigarette ends were dead he looked up to see there were still some people around. The Laurent-Chanel clock struck six p.m. He looked around and turned back: he was no longer interested in shops. His stomach had started to rumble, so the best thing to do was get a bite to eat. He walked to the end of the Galleria to the snack bar on the ground floor of the McDonald-Nestlé building. The band of musicians was still playing nonstop. He ordered a hot dog and a beer. The bar was half empty maybe because it wasn't dinner time yet. On Andrea's left was a business man in office attire busy working on his laptop while on his right was a group of boys greedily devouring numerous cheeseburgers. It was the same group he had seen previously getting off the *transport*. They saw Andrea and whispered something to each other but he didn't notice. He ate slowly staring into space and even if he was famished he chewed on every mouthful. At that moment Andrea wasn't really with it; he had got lost in his thoughts as they stormed his brain. He must have sat there for about an hour. When he was full he got up leaving half the hot dog on his plate. He paid the due sum and went out into the cold autumnal air of Milan.

The clock above the checkout said seven p.m. and there were fewer people around now. In less than an hour the Darkening alarm would go off and not many people would stay around to wait for the closing time of the *iperco-ops*. Andrea decided to get out of town down Via Torino, but he didn't want to go home just yet, not now that he felt he was finding answers to his problem. He wanted to be alone with his thoughts for a while longer maybe to understand his intuition better or maybe to overcome the unknown which tormented him. It was twenty to eight when Andrea reached Piazza Agostino. It had taken him a long time, not only because of his slow pace but also due to the various stops he had made. The districts were still not empty, but people now were hurrying on their way to be sure to be home before eight o clock. This last rush was due to the fact that after the Darkening there was a risk of bumping into the Men of the Night, a gang of vandals that enjoyed destroying everything and anything in their way as well as molesting innocent folk. The tabloids had named them the 'panic of darkness' and they were right in a sense as the people were really afraid to be outside away from home after dark in the cold core of the night. As soon as eight o'clock struck, all house and office lights were switched off immediately; a sharp whistle went off which could be heard through all the streets: it spread like a thick fog which enwrapped everyone. Light disappeared making way for a silent darkness. Andrea was taken by surprise and in a turn everyone around him had gone inside behind their apartment doors. His agitation brought him back to his senses and he also felt a bit shaky in his legs. He hadn't been out at night for ages, he wasn't used to it and the urban legends he had heard only increased this fear. Luckily there was the moon which improved visibility except for where the moon rays couldn't reach between the rows of high line apartment blocks. Andrea was lucky because nights like these were rare; a full moon didn't appear every night. Night time may have been so clear that you could even see the stars but they didn't offer enough light so they left everyone in total darkness: those so-called moonless nights encouraged delinquents. They were risky nights, nothing could be seen, nothing could be heard, absolutely nothing at all. Not even Andrea heard anything, not even the far off steps of those who were following him and had been doing so since he had left the snack bar. There were five or six of them dressed in grey so they naturally blended into the same grey gloom; they were ready to start a scuffle. Andrea unaware, continued on his way when he suddenly felt a hard hit at the back of his neck which threw him to the ground.

'Hey bastard, what the hell are you doing hanging around at this hour?' one of them said scoffing.

'Well, don't you know it could get dangerous?' said another voice coming from the same direction as the other one.

'Right let's see what you've got in your pockets, eh?' said the first voice.

Andrea vaguely heard them as two or three others continued to kick violently into his stomach. Andrea tried to lift his head but every time he just got yet another punch in the face. A hand went through his pockets but found nothing.

'Damn it!' said a second voice. 'This idiot has sod all! You thought he looked like easy game but he hasn't got a wallet nor credit cards – he's just a poor beggar! – either that, or he's stupid or he's being crafty!'

Another comment, another kick. There were some more exchanges but Andrea was now so dazed that he couldn't wait for it to be over. When it was finally over, he heard voices moving away and he lifted his eyes to see shadows running off down one of the alleys. They were skinheads and wore baggy jeans and grey velvet jackets. This was the second time he had seen them disappearing. He then heard the police alarm. He opened his eyes and found the strength to pick himself up; he had no intention of hanging around for the police. He didn't want to be accused of being out after hours and get a fine on his E-id card, which he had left at home any way. His stomach ached and blood was coming out of his mouth but he managed to reach the nearest alleyway. Andrea staggered toward a narrow street in complete darkness and even though he was limping he found safety behind a street cleaning machine parked there. The police patrol car cruised slowly past waving the search lights left and right like a light house that pans over the dark sea. It passed the alleyway without stopping; there was only the sound of a radio transmitter and nothing more. Andrea stood still in silence waiting until he could no longer hear the alarm meaning they were far off. He was safe now unless of course that alleyway was the safe house of those delinquents. It wasn't such a narrow alley after all but quite wide, wide enough for *transport*. He couldn't see the end. Maybe it was a dead end but it was his best shot seeing that the police were still patrolling the area. Drying the blood on his lip, he dragged himself up knocking the metal street cleaning machine with his back. The loud bang made a cat jump out from somewhere and it nearly jumped on Andrea who was already scared stiff. Andrea sighed in relief and carried on walking into the darkness. He remembered he was just a stone's throw from Piazza Agostino, but walking in total darkness it was easy to lose one's sense of direction. Andrea tried to think back to where he had left off but visibility was low and in every corner he thought he saw an image or object moving. Just when he was in one of these hallucinatory states he put his foot into a hole and fell face down onto the cold, dusty concrete. He put his hands over his face to save his fall so he didn't do himself any harm, just a slight pain in his foot which was stuck in the hole. Andrea could barely see anything let alone a hole, but from its shape he realised it wasn't a drain nor an uneven part of the street considering its depth. A bit of curiosity came over Andrea, so trying to forget his pain and injuries he crawled toward the opening. He put his hand inside fumbling and felt some rusty iron bars fixed onto one of the four walls. Was it an unusual stairway, seeing as the drains in Milan had an excellent maintenance? What was the difference? Not convinced Andrea decided to slip down into the hole, into an even darker abyss. The descent lasted a long time and then the darkness seemed to change; from the abyss came a shaft of light shining upward blinding Andrea's weak eyes, weak due to his length of time in darkness. The hole or rather the stairway ended in a horizontal tunnel   that was high and wide enough for an average man standing to pass through. The light came from what seemed to be a distant exit; it was a soft clear coloured light and it certainly wasn't an artificial one. Attracted by the dazzle Andrea began to move faster and faster without running though, without breaking the silence which still reigned. As he gradually got closer to the source of light, things, his clothes, his hands and the surrounding area took on a more definite shape. The side walls were made of brick and in their ancient splendour they must have been a colour similar to Siena earth but now they were covered in mould and cobwebs and had become a faded green colour. Several blocks of stone created a pavement which was covered in thick dust especially in the grooves but some long standing carvings were just slightly visible. Andrea didn't take much notice of this as he was more interested in getting to the end of the tunnel. His eyes were suffering; first his eyes dilated so much that they burnt due to too much time spent in darkness, then they adjusted to the strong light and he was able to grasp the scene with amazement.

A small rectangular room opened up in front of Andrea. It had a high ceiling, higher than the tunnel, about a meter higher with two pillars in the middle. Along the walls lots of candelabra held the same number of candles lighting the whole space. The two central pillars were ornate with relief work and decorations. Wooden furniture of the cheapest quality was everywhere, opaque glass bottles, heaps of waste paper littered everywhere, all covered in layers of dust. It looked a bit like Milan during the Recycling Years. The left wing of the room was empty except for a purple leather armchair that had seen better days as it was now worn and torn all over. On the right there was a writing desk with a few pieces of scribbled paper on it, a holder made of glass full of pens and a half used red candle. Two very simple file cabinets stood next to the desk and didn't match at all with the rich decoration of the two pillars. Above the three pieces of furniture was a shelf hanging from the wall weighed down by all the books on it. They nearly all had red rat eaten covers. Indeed we were now light years away from the time of books. Andrea had never been able to put his hands on a book as the Years of Change had transformed the way people learned. Now there were hundreds of online libraries and *ekletto-encyclopaedias*, not to mention the World Wide Web which held every possible piece of information. The network had changed forever every aspect of life, even though it hadn't changed much since the last century. Andrea knew one or two interesting essential facts: as a young boy he had done some research on the history of paper and he remembered papyrus, a city called Alexandria and a man called Gutenberg but he had never imagined a whole room full of books, spread everywhere almost as if it was impossible to grasp the essential information. Judging from the condition of the volumes of books on the shelves and the yellowed faded paper on the floor and desk the room had never seen the light of day. Whoever could live here in such a primitive and inadequate way? How long had this person lived underground, ignored by everyone? Andrea went up closer to the desk and glanced at the scribble but couldn't decipher any of the messages written among blobs of red wax and erasures. He glanced at the titles of the volumes but he had never heard of any of them. He was about to pen one of the cabinets when he suddenly felt something cold along his back and push against his ribs.

'Who on earth are you?' said a croaky voice in a threatening tone.

Andrea was immobilised, as he felt his assailant's weapon to be an iron bar. He decided the best thing was to do as he was told, but he wasn't sure whether to give his true identity or a false name.

'If I were you I would hurry up and speak young man!' the voice said in a feeble voice as he threateningly brandished his weapon, even if he did so with a slight tremble and uncertainty. The 'young man' also sounded unsuitable seeing as Andrea was over thirty five and had greyish hair unless his aggressor was older than him.

Andrea risked it and turned quickly to snatch the weapon. He was quick enough and managed to push his aggressor to the ground, throwing the weapon into the furthest corner of the room, then he looked carefully and in a way his guesswork about age was right. On the ground collapsed up against the column, trembling from head to foot was a grotesque looking old man with white hair. He was wearing a striped shirt and brown flannel trousers held up by braces: very badly dressed! Andrea was quite shocked by this old man as he was not used to seeing people of a certain age. Nowadays old people just weren't seen around; all over-seventies were confined to special institutions built for them in isolated country areas. Some people called them homes, especially those who were about to go and live there but their real name was *gerials*. No-one knew exactly where this word had come from, maybe it was from Greek. It had been a drastic solution taken to help reduce the pension problem. Indeed the idea of having a holiday village with all comforts was the right magnet to attract the over-seventies who were looking for peace and quiet in their old age. There were no old people in Milan any more so why was this man still here? Andrea had no idea; it took him all his courage to go near him and touch his wrinkled skin. It was a horrible sensation for Andrea because it was the first time he had ever seen such an old person. He made sure he wasn't armed as he got closer to him and stared at his face. The old man was still awake even if he was a bit shaken after his rather violent and unexpected fall.

'Are you alright?' asked Andrea slightly worried.

The old man opened his eyes and on seeing Andrea, he was petrified. He immediately crawled backward puffing and panting, opening his glassy eyes. Andrea stepped forward in an attempt to be friendly but at the same time he was getting impatient with the old man who had started shrieking at the top of his voice.

'No, I'm not going back there, not out there!'

He tried to find his weapon. Andrea looked around and saw it behind the chair. To his surprise that iron bar was actually a gun from the past century, something you just couldn't buy any more. This chap was a real museum piece too and just like any antiquity he had lost his lustre. Andrea knelt down to reach for the gun and saw the old man out of the corner of his eye as he tried to sit himself up against the column. He still held his arm up against his face but his watery eyes weren't covered. They were fixed on Andrea. They seemed to have a silvery grey twinkle which was the only remaining trace of a past youth and it just didn't seem possible that this weak melancholic man could once have been young like him.

'You still haven't answered my question: who on earth are you?' repeated the old man as soon as he had calmed down and was less threatening.

'Andrea Rossi!' said Andrea putting his hand out as a sign of friendship and peace. 'Pleased to meet you, despite the circumstances.'

'Have we already met?' asked the old man suspiciously.

'Not at all! I haven't a clue who you are.'

'Well, young man,' said the old man in a serious and challenging tone. 'You've come this far, catapulting yourself into my private stuff, you attack me...'

'Look, I believe it was you who attacked me.' interrupted Andrea. The old man took no notice as he wearily got back up onto his feet.

'I'm not going out there, forget it!' moaned the man.

'I don't understand. Can you explain where it is you don't want to go?' insisted Andrea. The old man turned slowly and stared questioningly.

'I don't want to go back into the world outside.' the old man replied in a faint voice. 'I don't want to live in a dead world where the mind and body no longer embrace each other.'

The old man turned back massaging his aching back with his hand. Andrea listened amazed. These last words spoken by the old man were yet another of those infinite clicks, like a gold key which opens the golden treasure. At last Andrea had come across someone who had manifested the same strange symptoms as he had symptoms of uneasiness and disgust toward today's society. He had had this unnatural malaise for years. Now he had found someone on the planet with his same problem and this someone he had found living in an underground basement right under the multinational skyscrapers of Milan. Curious of his discovery Andrea moved toward the old man who had already forgotten him and was busily tidying papers on his desk.

'Has it always been like this?' asked Andrea anxiously. 'Please, give me an answer.......it's important.'

Andrea wasn't quite sure what he was looking for, he just trusted his intuition in his search for something the world already had but he couldn't find. On hearing this imploration the old man stopped picking up paper and turned round again to offer his words of wisdom. He was now wearing a pair of glasses with gold rims and he had a serious and academic look about him. He stared into Andrea's eyes with a different expression, a more ordered and less confused one.

'Important?' said the old man severely. 'What do you mean by important, young man of the outside world?'

Andrea was stuck for words; he hadn't a clue what to say. This important thing he was talking about didn't refer to a concrete thought; he was quite unaware of the importance which had driven him to ask that question. Unfortunately his intuition stopped there and the old man could see he was at a loss for words. He didn't laugh but glared at him with a grin on his face.

'Oh, well you don't even know where to start.' he said the second time grinning. 'You and everyone else out there are all too ready and impatient to say something without reflecting on what is really important for you. Do you really think you are aware of your actions? Well, I'd like to say that today nobody stops to think and you confirm my theory.'

Andrea understood but didn't move. He didn't have the courage to talk and he also felt a sense of regret and anger that he had been put down by a damn oldie.

However the old man's words had moved strange sensations in him, pulsating his every part. There was a meaning in those words which let him forget time and space and even if Andrea tried he simply couldn't get anywhere.

'I want to understand.' said Andrea in a decisive tone.

The old man gave him a strange look turned his back on him as he bent over to open a desk drawer. From a pile of yellowed papers of all sizes came the famous red diary. The old man took it in his hand and gave it to Andrea in a friendly manner. Andrea hesitated at the old man's unexpected change of behaviour but then took the diary in both hands. As soon as he touched the velvet cover Andrea realised the old man was giving him a chance. He wouldn't have unveiled his secret for anything in this world because the antidote to his uneasiness lay in that miserable cubby-hole.

'You'll need this as well!' said the old man showing him a plastic pen with a blue top. Andrea recognised what it was from a photo he had seen in the *ekletto-encyclopaedia* and even if he was a bit unsure about this complicated instrument, he took it trusting completely in that old man who he had found revolting in every way up to a moment ago. It might have been his desire to understand that had convinced the old man but it seemed incredible that everything had happened with very few words, just simple gestures. He walked back silently towards the corridor but before going over the threshold the old man spoke for the last time; his words opened Andrea's mind for a second time.

'You need that to jot down your thoughts.'

Andrea nodded and without saying more he disappeared into darkness.

In a couple of minutes Andrea was back in the deserted streets, back in the real world shrouded by darkness of unconsciousness. He had lost track of time but the lights of the *iperco-ops* were still on and he managed to get home thanks to the last *transport* which came past along the dark road. The clock over the driver's seat said nine fifty. It was almost closing time so the last people were racing to get a seat on the last transport; of course it wasn't a mad dash like in the rush hour or on holidays when folk fought to be safe from the Men of the Night. Andrea sat down quietly feeling pleased while on the other side of the window the world seemed exactly the same. The encounter with the old man had been a turning point, an unexpected turning point on a cold November day.

II

The alarm clock went off at seven sharp when all Milan and all the other Italian metropolises woke up after the Darkening. Andrea woke up feeling half asleep as per usual: his sleepless night had ended five hours ago but at least it hadn't lasted all night. His room was still in half-darkness but the light of dawn had brightened the sky and from the tops of the large apartment blocks you could see the brightness spreading delicately over the sky. The sun was somewhere behind the large apartment blocks where it had always been and where it had been forgotten by man. Andrea got out of bed to the repetitive sound of the liquid crystal alarm clock and he wouldn't have minded going back out into the Darkening. He looked around with his eyes still half open and heavy, trying to find his way to the bathroom just like every morning but his eyes ended up looking at his desk. The candle had worn out on its own; the diary was still where he had left it open at the fourth page with the pen next to it. It hadn't been much use in improving his mental state. Andrea was about to close it but before doing so out of curiosity he looked to see what he had actually written. Nothing special. Just a simple summary of his meeting with the old man that he probably wouldn't even remember after a week. He yawned out of boredom with the previous night's events; he thought it was another day wasted. He glanced up at the clock to see it was already quarter past seven. As he did this, the diary page lifted as if blown over by the whiff of a magical wind. Andrea read the next page, page five, and his eyes widened. In the centre of the page was some writing highlighted in cubical characters.

No-one ever stops to think
No-one ever stops to think

No-one ever stops to think
I am so different from you.

Andrea almost collapsed. The old man's words which up to a week ago held something magic were now a nightmare, a terrible nightmare that had made him behave badly and write ignoble things typical of a silly person who didn't use his head. He regretted discovering that hiding place; last night had confirmed his behaviour was bad and troubled. He needed a holiday, that's what he needed. Andrea put the diary down and went to the bathroom to rinse his face and rid himself of his thoughts.

In the meantime the automatic lights came on as programmed, together with all the others in the Belfiore apartment block. The sharp click almost blinded Andrea as he felt the light entering his eyes like a sting. He shut his eyes automatically as the words 'I am different to you' echoed in his head .The flash of light had brought a flash to his brain reminding him. The water hadn't woken him and he couldn't do anything. Awake but troubled he went into the kitchen to get his clothes hanging on the chair. His kitchen was tidy maybe because there wasn't much to keep tidy nor was there much food to eat in the cupboards. He rarely had lunch or dinner at home; the *iperco-ops* always had something good on sale and the pleasure of not having to cook and be served persuaded almost everyone. He would have had his meals out today too but first he had a coffee to get rid of his sleepiness. The coffee machine was ready, the beans were hot and ready and had a much better effect than Alberoni's decaffeinated pills. He drank the strong dark liquid in a couple of sips then went back into the main room to tidy his bed and other stuff. The white shirt he had put on was slightly creased but there wasn't time to get his Decreaser out. It was now half past seven so Andrea thought it was time to get a move on. The *transport* always arrived on time at seven thirty five with not many people aboard. At this time of day there was little risk of a crowded bus so Andrea climbed on freely. He wasn't carrying anything bulky because everything was in his E-id, and the E-id was everything. He could do everything with this card; buy, sell, pay for his transport, access his database; most of his social life was compacted into this plastic card with its microchip. Andrea used it to open the glass door of his office which was in the high skyscraper Fichampon.

It was a large square building and once the headquarters of the Exhibition Fiera Campionaria in Milan but now it belonged to the Firm. It was quite an old structure divided up into several different sectors. The main body formed the central skyscraper or rather the Cedir that regulated all mechanisms in Milan, according to Global Corp. directives. From this cylindrical tower a labyrinth of stairways and corridors led to the various sectors of the Fichampon and hundreds of ultra clean offices where the clerks of the twenty first century were busy working at their computers.

Andrea's working day began at eight just as he had programmed. The Firm allowed its workers to choose their hours of work but they had to start at eight once or twice a week. However, the possibility to organize working hours in whatever way you wished meant you could always get a few free hours. The only downside was that there were requests for overtime by the Firm which could be a real nuisance if your workload ended at four p.m. Naturally it all depended on the work to be done and by the people involved. The payment remained the same: a sum of E -credit deposited into the Net-Bank- Code, which had very quickly and easily done away with cash and other financial worries. Nobody moaned about having some kind of economical help; everybody had a sum of E-credit that was more than sufficient to get by on. However there were still a few big fish who had accumulated large amounts due to their careers but they had never stolen money from anyone. Indeed it wasn't Andrea who had paid that vampire of a psychologist; the receipts were sent directly to the Firm. In this way the world had progressed and poverty had become history. Andrea had read in his *ekletto-encyclopaedia* that the working world had changed greatly and had modernised in every sector and had taken on the name of Egonomics. This 'economy of I' allowed people to take out an agreement between the *e-preneur* (young entrepreneurs or managers with excellent ideas for new projects) and the *venture capitalist* (investors of Global Corp with special funds to finance and participate in company projects). The agreement came through the Dot-Com System, a means of communication for rapid investment via the Internet. The so-called marriage between ideas and capital were based on an intense E-commerce and gave people the chance to carry out one's work from home, negotiating business on the network and creating new projects on line. At this point home became one's world or rather one's castle but you were fully linked to the outside world. Obviously office work had almost disappeared but some *office centres* still existed that required technicians to answer the needs of Global Corp. or check the working of every city infrastructure. In Italy the *office centres* was called 'Compagnia' just like in every other country; for example, Firm in the UK or Selskab in Denmark. Both the E-commerce and the *office centres* were run by the almighty Global Corp. that governed the market and was always on the lookout for new proposals from every corner of the earth. Unfortunately the market had its rules and not everyone could be part, great talent in management were required and Andrea just didn't consider himself up to it. He had taken part in the virtual master course in Turin for admission into the scientific field, but he wasn't up to the standard compared to others, so he became a *data miner*, and anyway it wasn't hard work nor badly paid, on the contrary there was a climate of autonomy and light-heartedness. Its only defect was that it didn't offer any career, it didn't offer any progress. A *data miner*'s job was to extract useful bit for the Firm from the long, boring lists of superfluous data as they accumulated over the years. This data was about registered surveys in certain cities and they could be figures or references regarding trade or consumption of electrical energy or the birth rate and so on. It was the Firm that then decided which advantageous points to highlight to Global Corp., but this was the job of the IPO*counter*. It was a perfect system and it didn't undermine your social place nor your health; all its members were important pillars in the Global Corp., synchronised and ready to earn a lot with minimum work.

The neon lights came on with a simple contact with an E-id chip and the Fichampon circuit. The office shone in light grey on all its walls. The monochromatic monotony was broken by two hung framed abstract pictures and two vases placed near the entrance. There was a sign over the glass door which was present in all the offices: a sign written in large black cubic letters which contrasted with the pale grey. The position chosen was meant to highlight the motto of the Company that every worker read on entering.

He who stops is lost.

Andrea walked in without turning, plunged into his chair made of fake black leather, and as he wished to finish the backlog of work, he quickly inserted his E-id into the hard drive on his left. The hard drive was for clocking in at work and also enabled you to access certain tools on your personal desk. Both the glass door and the desk screened your E-id to prevent strangers entering.

Once your code was recognised by the system, the desk lit up highlighting the smoky grey surface. At first it appeared empty but it really hid all the most advanced tools including a *digital-desktop* in the middle and a digital communicator on the right for vocal or visual internal communications at the Fichampon. There was a space near the drive for mini discs, cell phones and other personal objects but Andrea kept it empty because he didn't like leaving things in the office even if it was totally safe. He actually kept his cell phone at home for the simple reason that it was too old and couldn't compete with the latest WAP Coloured Hologram 1600. Andrea glanced at the box then turned to his *digital-desktop* pressing the icon #2743 with his finger. A large window opened up straightaway covering the whole aqua blue background of the screen and a long list of last week's data came up in front of his half-awake eyes. It took a while to finish, the numbers scrolled down endlessly without stop, so fast that they made Andrea open his eyes. This rapid, non-stopping movement made him remember a phrase that he had almost forgotten but was still there in his brain. 'No-one stops to think anymore'. This is what Andrea read on his *digital-desktop* instead of words. Indeed the numbers weren't figures but data and dates indicating years, months and days in the future. Once more the date had struck him, once again the passing of time had troubled him, just like the previous evening, leaving him perplexed, lost, in a confused flow of images and words. Andrea realised he had a stupid expression on his face and it was a bit risky to be seen staring into space and doing nothing but he couldn't do anything to stop it as the concept of passing of time was far more interesting. It was a loud voice that convinced him to let the image slide and come back to reality; it was an unmistakable voice, known by everyone here at the Fichampon.

'Rossi, a bit more discipline and less time wasting!'

His voice was always thunderous when it blurted out of the cables of the digital communicator and every time he pronounced those five words they sounded like magic words worthy of admiration. He didn't usually say anything else, the announcement stopped suddenly and the digital communicator went dead. But this time Andrea saw him in flesh and blood (well, sort of!) through the holographic projection on his digital communicator. Andrea looked at his CEO seriously and put on an expression of a constantly diligent worker in an attempt to hide his absent mind.

'Rossi,' communicated the CEO trying to make the situation clearer. 'As you know the Compagnia is made up of strong, sturdy pillars. These pillars are qualified to do an easy, safe job and the success of Global Corp depends on them, keeping in mind that we are just a small part of this world organization. If we work slowly we are going to slow down the whole group and if we can't keep the pace with the others we will risk destabilising the whole system. The other day you were asked to find data relevant to transgenic corn in the last semester. Such an easy assignment wasn't completed so I felt I had to call you via holographic projection, given the seriousness of the circumstances.'

'Director,' murmured Andrea with reverence. 'The data has been found and I was going to forward it to you this morning.'

Andrea realised he was in the CEO's bad books. If he made such an appearance, some negative observation could be expected as all positions were assigned via S-mail while compliments were given at the virtual conferences. There was no great risk as dismissals were a thing of the past and the Firm helped you to get back on track as soon as possible. Naturally Andrea regarded himself as an exceptional case after so many failed attempts but these continuous scolds by the CEO were strange and repetitive: he couldn't always remember what the conversations were about, the only thing he remembered was him calling out his surname and his faults at work. Andrea wasn't frightened and didn't feel in danger because these comments were frequent so he just carried on behaving in the same way, handing in data that was non-existent. In the CEO's eyes Andrea had improved so he remained safe but he didn't know what would happen to him if he did go over the limit and he didn't know anyone who had gone over it. Who could he talk to about it? It was a rare thing, perhaps the first in the history of mankind, or maybe only a small flame in the dark universe.

'Rossi,' continued the CEO in a different tone, less thunderous and calmer, more understanding. 'I intend to have the data by this afternoon but maybe first you should make your way to the second floor of the Cedir. You know what I am talking about I presume, don't you?'

Andrea did know what he meant by this. He was talking about the Knowledgeer, an enormous computer situated on the second floor of the central tower at the Fichampon. Nothing awesome, just artificial intelligence made in Germany and capable of translating experience into software code so as to classify someone according to the correct ranking. Everyone who wished to enter the Fichampon had to pass through the Knowledgeer first. The procedure was simple and it didn't involve much as the scanner did all the work screening your brain matter and elaborating the results thus determining your role in the Firm without any such thing as an interview. Andrea had already been screened and had ended up as a *data miner*. He was happy with that but in those moments when he stopped for just a few minutes to look at something he was writing or started thinking, he didn't find any satisfaction with what he was doing.

'I'm on my way now!' answered Andrea trying to show interest in the problem. 'Give me time to send the data I have already gathered on my *digital-desktop*.'

'Take your time, Rossi."

And with the same quickness he had appeared, he disappeared as his image faded from over the desk. Andrea gazed into space for a moment and the turned to get back to his work so as not to waste any more time. In front of him was a long list about overproduction of transgenic tomatoes so he considered sending this data up. The consequences didn't really matter but it was important to save his face with the CEO and send something. Who knows why he wanted him to be screened by the Knowledgeer, maybe to check there were no mental imbalances even if the doctors had already confirmed so. Even if he wasn't really worried, now he had to send this data and get ready to face the sitting .He wanted to read his electronic mail but seeing there was little time he'd better not keep the CEO waiting. While the drive sent the data, Andrea tried to relax. He sat down in his armchair and shut his eyes to think about the CEO, his problems, the diary and the meeting with the old man. All these things seemed to be linked strangely enough, like a chain. It was a feeling, a premonition; until a few minutes ago the morning torment had bogged him down, perhaps because he always tried to understand what was happening to him, well knowing the consequences. Andrea concentrated and the sentence 'No-one stops to think anymore' came to mind. He had the puzzle of images and memories before him and he became more worried than before. He looked at the sign above the door which he had hardly ever considered until now and read it carefully. 'He who stops is lost'. The letters seemed to jumble themselves up and thoughts filtered through his eyes. Andrea started to read 'He who thinks is lost' and he repeated to himself 'No-one ever stops to think'.

The second floor of the Cedir could be reached by walking along a moving walkway linked to Corridor C. The rooms and corridors were still quiet because from eight to nine there were never many people: the only people present were the ones who had chosen that particular day to work. So it was a rare thing to bump into someone at that hour. The Fichampon was also so big that it was difficult to ever see a group of people together amid thousands of offices. Andrea came to the end of the walkway and stopped in front of a large metallic door. This was the entrance to the second floor occupied exclusively by the Knowledgeer and nothing else, not even a lift linking it to the upper floors of the Cedir. The room behind the large door was circular like an arena, with a blue platform in the centre and a chair on it. The candidate sat here under the threatening point of the Knowledgeer. The point was an upside down cone which projected its laser beam into the candidate's brain. All around there were hundreds of seats facing the majestic machine. Andrea was surprised because it had been sixteen years since his last visit here. He remembered the mass of multi- coloured cables which ran under plastic strips and re appeared through holes in the floor and walls. That cybernetic web no longer existed, technology had reduced the size of the processors and the Knowledgeer was no longer big and bulky as it had been designed originally. The room where the Knowledgeer stood was empty now. The last series of candidates had passed through the week before and the Firm had just started intense production. The next selection would be in a week's time. The Knowledgeer was also put to use for occasions like the one Andrea was about to face.

As soon as he got up onto the platform, the *dvd-screen* light nearby lit up to show the CEO's face clearly. The clock on the right corner of the screen displayed nine o'clock just to prove how punctual the CEO always was. The head of the Firm was a good person; he embraced all the absolute values a worker should have and made whoever worked for the Firm proud. No-one had ever seen him in flesh and blood as they say, he was seen in photos, in the digital cathode tubes which were enough to make his image so neat and clear that he seemed real and concrete. Andrea turned to appreciate his confident smile and in reply the CEO asked Andrea to sit himself down on the reclining chair.

'Well, Rossi' said the CEO clearing his voice. 'Let's get on with this. I have other business to attend to. The scanner will be very quick; it's a re-elaboration programme capable of checking your data file. Get into position, please.'

All the CEO's hard work was admirable, in the past there had never been such a busy head of department and not even such an altruist president. Andrea could only admire these qualities and get ready for the test.

'Ready?' added the CEO.

'Ready, sir!' answered Andrea keeping his eyes fixed on the point of the upside down cone.

Suddenly a green light flashed about a span from his brain while the strange machine over him lit up with a series of intermittent lights. Andrea shut his eyes slightly to withstand the intensity of the light, and then he shut them tightly to unwind the tension. Soon after, he fainted as if he was under the effect of an anaesthetic. The last thing he felt was a stroke, something warm, then emptiness and warmth again. He opened his eyes after about five minutes; five minutes which Andrea didn't remember living. In a flash the scanner had filtered into his brain catching old and new data and at the same time the CEO had re- elaborated his data card.

'Interesting, Mr. Rossi.' commented the CEO 'There's no change. Your problem was something very simple, there was no need for doctors or psychologists. The computer here shows that your level of concentration is the only value below the normal, twenty-five per cent to be precise. I think a day or two's rest is the best thing for you.'

'Do I have to go to see the psychologist or can I cancel my appointment?' asked Andrea rubbing his eyes.

'I will inform Mr. Vazzano of your progress. However, I advise you to go to the sitting for one last time. I hope to see you in my office in three days in top form.'

'I can't wait.' said Andrea in a friendly manner although he still couldn't believe concentration was the cause of all his problems.

The CEO said goodbye and switched off the *dvd-screen*, without expecting any questions from Andrea. Such a quick check up confused him and even surprised him. Concentration! It was probably low but what was the cause then? Why couldn't Andrea work or sleep or even live? Strange questions to which there was no answer but Andrea continued to ask himself and it worried him. There was nothing else to do but leave the Knowledgeer behind him, a machine that had already forgotten the matter although it had registered all on its database. The questions instead continued to roll around inside Andrea's head.

Outside the room there were more people moving around the corridors now. The chance of bumping into someone you knew was minimal in a building that housed over ten thousand clerks, but the flow of people cheered the empty spaces in the Fichampon. Andrea didn't pay attention to the faces of those passing by, especially now that he had got into the habit of walking with his head down absorbed in his deep problems. Most times it was the others who noticed him among the crowd. Just when he was waiting for the lift to go back to the office a pat on the shoulder made him turn around. The clean shaven face and smiling face of Filippo Alberoni was right before him.

'Good morning, colleague!' exclaimed Alberoni showing how friendly he was using his usual formula.

Andrea couldn't stand him nor his automatic and repetitive phrases. Ever since he had known him it had been impossible to get rid of him; it wasn't his habit to avoid a person who was attached to him in a certain way but deep inside every part of him, eaten away by his enigmatic sickness, there was a strange strength which wanted to drive him away, even kick him, shout at him and even swear. Andrea shivered and tried to keep this feeling at bay so that it wasn't evident.

'Everything alright Andrea?' asked Alberoni rather worried. 'Do you want a decaffeinated coffee pill?'

Andrea couldn't care less how worried Alberoni was, also because at times it was just an excuse to make a scene and the pill was a good way.

'Fine, no pill thanks.' he answered quickly.

'It's ages since I last saw you, eh? It must be a week at least. Did you get my S-mail?'

Alberoni had no intention of stopping his conversation; he saw this as an opportunity to talk to Andrea who as per usual didn't have the guts to end it. Maybe Alberoni didn't even perceive how Andrea wanted to get away but where was Andrea to go now that he was technically on holiday?

'What S-mail?!' continued Andrea partly curious and partly irritated. 'Sorry but I haven't had time this morning to check my incoming mail.'

'I see. Anyway it wasn't anything important. Only a message to let you know I intend to return to the Sperm Bank and, seeing as you came with me last time, I wondered if you were interested in coming with me again. What do you say?'

His 'no' was already ready on the tip of his tongue as soon as the name Sperm Bank was mentioned and as usual body and mind split in two opposite sides until his body prevailed.

'Yes, tell me when.'

Andrea's voice expressed reluctance but Alberoni didn't grasp it out of euphoria, pleased Andrea had accepted. A man full of himself saw the others as a means of support, that's what he was and the more Andrea thought about it the more he felt used. He always had this sensation when he spoke to Alberoni but it was so subtle and well hidden as not to be recognised. Often with the feeling of exploitation came doubt, such a strong doubt which made Andrea close up on himself. He was not capable of facing the external world and expressing his opinions. Anyway, how could Andrea be sure Alberoni was using him given that more than once his intuition had not worked?

'Great!' exclaimed Alberoni with his usual white smile. 'I'll come and pick you up with my tandem on Thursday afternoon. Is that alright?'

Andrea could see the joy in his eyes but noticed the hesitation in his voice. Surely uncertainty was equal to lies.

'No, Thursday I've got a visit with my psychologist.' answered Andrea hoping to block Alberoni's false pleasure, and emphasised the word 'psychologist' to make it sound serious. Surprised by his answer, Alberoni stood silent for a while undecided on how to answer but his reaction was different to what Andrea expected.

'With the psychologist? What on earth has happened since I last saw you?'

Alberoni's expression took on a worried air again but this time Andrea didn't see the hesitation of before. The passage from happy to sad was natural so the feeling was spontaneous. How was it possible that only a moment before he had lied so easily? Perhaps he hadn't lied about him or maybe he was just clever at making the false appear true. Andrea again fell into doubt and felt some shame for doubting a person who may only have wanted to be friendly. He had never been so suspicious towards people then all of a sudden he turned into a monster. Andrea's body spoke again without listening to the cry from his brain.

'Never mind dear Alberoni. Listen, why don't we meet up on Friday afternoon, OK? See you soon!'

Then a 'ding' announced the lift arriving on their floor and Andrea jumped in without waiting for his colleague. The doors closed straightaway and Andrea leant against the metallic wall and took a sigh of relief. He stood there in the corner with his eyes closed reflecting on the previous conversation; the gentle electronic rumble accompanied him in his thoughts as the lift went up to the upper floors. He didn't feel alone; there wasn't that air of silence that Andrea had been searching for but the insistent and oppressing sound of the external world, which with its sharp 'din don' brought Andrea to his floor and out of his thoughts. He walked down the corridor as far as his office without looking around, he didn't want to see anybody. Alberoni's face was still impressed on him, a face standing between true and false, between regret and light-heartedness. He plunged into his office chair keeping his eyes open this time, staring at the office entrance expecting Alberoni. He wanted to apologise, to explain himself but he didn't come and Andrea could do nothing but forget the whole matter. The *digital-desktop* clock showed nine forty a.m. The best thing to do to kill time until ten o'clock was prepare some of next week's work. The icon #2744 flashed on the screen and yet another list opened up with the same impetus as before. Andrea tried to pick out something undistinguishable and uniform in the list as it scrolled down.

At the end Andrea was forced to leave at eleven something. The Firm had admired his efforts by sending him another file of data and there was no way he could refuse seeing as he would soon have two days of doing absolutely nothing. Indeed Andrea felt better as soon as he was out of the Fichampon, his work had sent him into oblivion and now the fresh air made him feel free. There were two exits from the Fichampon, one which led out onto an internal square and the other led to a side street. Andrea always left from the latter as it was the best one to avoid the crowd mingling in the internal square, especially at this particular time of day when any meeting was a nightmare which made his condition worse. Andrea didn't want to make the same mistake he had made before with Alberoni so he preferred to slip out unnoticed and he stopped to catch the transport in Via Domodossola. He had a couple of plans for the afternoon some shopping and maybe a visit to the CRS but he didn't know what to do in the two hours before lunchtime. He gave it a thought accompanied by the electronic sound of the *transport* as it travelled at a fast speed through the Milan streets toward the centre. There were a lot of people around, not as many as in Piazza Duomo however, where about two million inhabitants passed per day, that is about half of the Milanese population. Andrea noticed the difference as the *transport* stopped in front of the cathedral. The crowd was there in the large square together with the pigeons standing still as if they had never moved. It didn't matter who the people were; it was always the same crowd as the yesterday and the day before that. Andrea got off the *transport* and walked among the crowd becoming a part of it. He was heading for the McDonald-Nestlé building. A bit of Internet surfing before lunch wasn't a bad idea and with all the Internet Cafés he would surely have found a vacant seat, as long as he avoided any crowds. He made his way to the top floors where there would be fewer people (lots of people couldn't be bothered to go so far up when the lower floors were more convenient). One of the Internet Cafes on the twelfth floor was almost empty and he could have a drink in peace. The café was painted an azure blue and on every wall, including the entrance, there was a 3D version of the globe which rotated on itself with the words 'Internet Café'. Andrea chose   a table near the large window. He hated the noise of the globe as it turned, it was unbearable like the noise in the lift. For the third time he fell into a chair but his body and mind were more relaxed as he was sure there was no CEO ready to disturb his relax time. He put his hand in his pocket and took out his E-id to insert into the drive placed on the desk and after pressing a couple of keys the order was sent and Andrea could enjoy a nice cup of cappuccino and brioche in front of the Time website. The headlines, written in bold, shouted.

Pegasus announces 90% stability

Another confirmation from the infinity of space. Pegasus was the space station built on Mars in 2031. Man had been on the red planet now for several years living between the canyons and deserts and was about to become completely independent from Cape Canaveral. The mission had started in 2015 by a company called NASA which sent space vehicles carrying special reactors. The objective was to pump the atmosphere into the reactor to put the carbon dioxide into contact with the hydrogen. At this point they obtained methane, water and oxygen which could be used to aid the arrival of the crew. After numerous tests, the shuttle Pegasus and its crew finally managed to land without any problems in May 2018. Building an earth habitat was a slow process but with the transfer of NASA to GASA funds increased and lost time was made up. Man had made another step toward the conquest of space and naturally it wasn't the only destination; there was also the Moon and the ISS (International Space Station) which played an important role .The former had become a rubbish dump after the Years of Recycling, an idea which hadn't met with resistance and had guaranteed clean cities; the latter was a scientific centre but also a holiday destination for tourists who wanted to have a holiday with no gravity for a few weeks.

Andrea didn't really follow all the developments of this space odyssey. These last few weeks had made him blind and dumb, forcing him to isolate himself. When would this nightmare end? He looked away from the screen and glanced out of the window trying to think about something else. From the twelfth floor he couldn't see Piazza Duomo and the view was limited to the lower floors of the Amazon-Virgin while higher up, beyond the twentieth floor of the New Microsoft-Sony, the blue sky with fluffy clouds reigned over the wonders of man with an air of indifference. Who knows what the astronauts see from up there, thought Andrea, perhaps they see confused masses like those in Piazza Duomo and they can't do other than watch from the other side of the infinite darkness of the universe.

'It would be great to visit ISS!'

A voice interrupted Andrea's thoughts again and he began to feel annoyed by these continuous interruptions. This time he would let them have it, Vazzano or Alberoni or whoever it was. He paused before turning to think what to say, but as soon as he had done so, he had to regret his words. It wasn't a nuisance standing in front of him but the nicest person out of all those he could meet at that time.

'Marco!' exclaimed Andrea forgetting all his bad thoughts. 'Marco Gandolfi, I'm so pleased to see you again. Take a seat.'

'Thanks. I hope I'm not disturbing you but I saw you here reading the latest news and I decided to come and see you.'

'You did the right thing.' answered Andrea and pointed to the screen. 'A trip in the cosmos wouldn't be a bad idea, eh?"

'Why don't you go? You know prices aren't as high as '58, don't you?'

'Of course I know. I remember when we there waiting for the prices to change.'

Andrea had a sudden flashback of his early years after the orphanage when he met Marco for the first time during the intercontinental video announcement of the first tourist trip into space. That happy moment seemed far off now even if he was only seventeen years old.

'Yeah, with our eyes fixed onto the *dvd-screen* and our dreams held in our hands. Today one of Man's many dreams has come true and there aren't many dreams left.'

Marco paused.

'But tell me, why don't you fancy going to see the ISS?'

In the meantime he had pressed one or two keys to order a hot chocolate.

'I didn't say I don't fancy it. It's just that lately I haven't felt up to a trip to the Canaries, never mind the ISS! What about you? I thought you had gone away somewhere because last week I was looking for you without any luck. Canaries or ISS?"

Marco paused before answering Andrea.

'I went to see my parents.'

Andrea's expression changed completely out of embarrassment for a question which was a bit indiscreet. He had forgotten that Marco was an old type, one of the few left in the world who had a mum and a dad. Gradually this generation was disappearing making way for test tube babies, the children of the Firm, and family were a thing of the past. Andrea regarded himself as a hybrid, an in-between of the two generations, between the natural and the artificial. Such a kind of fertilisation didn't mean diversity, both had integrated without difficulty, without discrimination. To tell the truth it was hard to tell the difference, to recognize who was born naturally from who was an embryo in a fridge cell but Andrea did perceive a slight difference, difficult to put his finger on, but nevertheless, there was something different. He often saw a strange twinkle in Marco's eyes like the twinkle of a dew drop, he often saw in him a melancholic expression which only lasted a moment then disappeared leaving room for a serene face. This was the difference, such a subtle difference that there was no plausible explanation. Anyway Andrea was sure this anomaly had made him different from the others, more accessible in a way and Andrea had taken advantage of this on more than one occasion to talk about his doubts and uncertainties and more than once Marco had been of assistance. Andrea admired his way of doing things, he behaved correctly towards him and now that he was going through a moment of crisis he was sure Marco would be able to help him. He wasn't like Alberoni, he wasn't like the others; with him, you could talk about certain things, without any problems or misunderstandings. Talking about his old kind of youth and his parents had put Andrea at ease; he remembered good and bad times, at the orphanage his first meeting with the Knowledgeer, and as he tried to go further back in time, events seemed to be faded in the fog of time, a fog that at this present time persecuted him day and night, reminding him of those dark years of a childhood gone by too quickly. He remembered the old man he had met the week before in that hiding place;

well, he had certainly lived his life to the full and who knows what kind of past it had been, probably very different from his own and probably better. At that moment Andrea went back to his melancholic world and felt the hurt inside, deep down inside without really knowing where it hurt, maybe his head, or his heart, maybe his lungs…

'They are well and say hello! How are things with you?'

The tone used by Marco in the two phrases was completely different and Andrea realised it was this precise moment that bewitched him, that twinkle, that change in expression, lively and intense. Of course he didn't have the courage to ask, it would be a silly question. However, he intended to carry on the same line of thought. He knew he could count on Marco. He knew he could find answers to his questions. He wasn't sure about how to set about putting the question but he was ready to take the step despite his total confusion. It was just a question of finding the right moment.

'Nothing special at the moment.' answered Andrea. 'Today I went to work and they gave me a few days off.'

'Really?' exclaimed Marco. 'You're lucky; I'm forced to work from home and can never rest. Do you know what I mean?'

'How come?'

'I've got to finish a project. I wanted to finish it before leaving but I didn't manage to so now I have to catch up.'

Marco worked as an architect and he was good at his job especially at times when building skyscrapers was a profitable business. Andrea admired him for this but in this precise moment it annoyed him. He didn't want to talk about work, he didn't want to be reminded of where he worked, his office, the corridors of the Fichampon, that place which for the first time appeared poky, for no precise reason.

'Are your parents in the *gerial* on the Lake of Como?" asked Andrea trying to get back to the previous conversation.

'Yes, they've been there ages now.'

Andrea heard the word 'ages', such an insignificant word but always involved with the turbine of time. Was this the right moment?

'Listen Marco…'

'Yes?' said Marco lifting up his eyes from his hot smoking cup.

Andrea stared at him straight in the eyes but he didn't have the courage, he didn't feel he could just break in out of nowhere to ask a question that could just be forgotten. He didn't have to get anyone else involved.

'Nothing.' said Andrea lowering his eyes over his cup of cappuccino.

This wasn't nor the time nor the place. He waited for Marco to speak before lifting his eyes.

'What are you doing in the next few days?' asked Marco sipping his brown liquid.

Andrea had to think before answering. To tell the truth Andrea had never had to spend two whole days without working. Nowadays work and free time got mixed up continually according to the principles of Egonomics, and to have free time without any work put Andrea in an awkward position, one he couldn't imagine himself in. Thank goodness his afternoon was already planned but he hadn't a clue about what to do after that for the next few days. Of course if he were more like all the others, without a brain sickness, he might not have found it necessary to invent a problem, but there was a sense of ill-being which would have forced him to stay house bound alone, because he simply wasn't able to bear company or rather crowds at the CRS. A holiday on the Canaries would be much better, one of those types of holidays arranged by the Firm at the end of the month. Last time, in October, he had chosen not to go, but now he couldn't wait for the 30th November. Then Marco asked him another question.

'Did you see the announcement?' said Marco pointing to the screen. '"The day after tomorrow reserve, but Saturday 20th November the Day of Light". Where will we end up if we carry on like this…?'

The phrase ended suspended and Andrea caught sight of his melancholic face for a second time, like a digital photo taken on the spur of the moment. It was a kind of nervous attitude, rather like the panic attack Andrea had been through a couple of hours ago in the lift. What did this have to do with the announcement? The Day of Light was a world day festival set up at the same time as the Darkening and it was the only day in the year when the streets all over the world were lit up for the whole night. Everyone waited eagerly for it after months of darkness. The date wasn't fixed beforehand and sometimes Global Corp. allowed two days instead of just one or even three or four. What was strange about this? Once again Andrea recognised a new and interesting quality in Marco which partly reflected some of his own attitudes and for this reason he was again attracted to him.

'Excuse me, but what do you mean when you say "where will we end up if we carry on like this…?"' asked Andrea convinced he had hit on the nail, but Marco continued talking without showing any signs of panic.

'What I mean is that petrol isn't a renewable energy source.'

'So? Everyone knows that, it's nothing new.'

'Well then, tell me why they still talk about the Day of Light while we are using up tons and tons a day of black gold.'

'I think we can afford it and anyway there are alternative sources.'

'Enough to satisfy the needs of the whole world?' said Marco in an austere tone.

'Look, I have never pressed a button that hasn't worked.' responded Andrea.

'Not yet, but it could happen.'

'Huh, who knows if and when it'll happen.'

Andrea's reply left Marco furious, furious at giving his opinion and then be contradicted immediately. He scowled and Andrea didn't know how to behave. In a sense he did agree with what Marco had said, in fact during his adventure during the Darkening he had given thought to the idea of having absolutely no electricity, but then he found it easier not to think about it.

'Forget about it, let's not argue about these stupid things.' said Andrea to soften the atmosphere.

'No,' responded Marco. 'You can't forget about it, you can choose not to argue about it but you can't forget it and call it an idiocy.'

You could see from Marco's face how angry he was. It was a reaction different to the one Andrea had expected. Marco may have been stronger in character compared to him who had brushed off Alberoni with such ease. Now he was trying to hide himself from Marco's inquisitive expression, yet again forced to hide away, aware of the divide between his understanding and his expression, aware that he was very sensitive and rarely spoke, and when he did he often said the wrong thing.

'Sorry.' said Marco throwing his coffee cup into the bin near the table. 'I didn't want to attack you like that but I take some things a bit too seriously. Well, I'd better be off. We'll be in touch.'

He got up and before leaving he shook Andrea's hand as a sign of friendship. He was still scowling and Andrea still saw that melancholic expression hidden in a mysterious mask. His handshake was so strong that it seemed alive, and then he left disappearing along the corridors outside the Internet Café, leaving Andrea just like he had left Alberoni outside the lift. The other customers on the premises muttered freely without a flinch. They had been both blind and deaf to their animated conversation but still holding the power of speech.

After lunch in a Steak House a few floors down, Andrea called in at the CRS. The Centre of Recreational Services was a section of the Amazon-Virgin that offered the most varied of pastimes, such as a virtual cinema, virtual relax and of course virtual video games which led to the masses of Milanese youth flocking there. The word 'virtual' appeared on every screen, on every wall and every adhesive strip stuck onto all the interactive machines until they hammered their way into your head and became a part of your life. The big advantage of this centre was its capacity to open up to a new completely personalised world where the stressed could relax, the tiny tots could have fun and the wild ones could get their taste of pure adrenalin. A way to let off steam carefree and worry-free, a way to get back on track, and Andrea who had stress enough to share, had opted for a break in the Tropics before his real holiday.

The Relax department on the fifth floor wasn't overcrowded and the only thing he really wished for was a moment of relax far away from daily life, lying in a hammock rocking in the tropical breeze. He inserted his E-id in the driver next to the deck chair, as the handbook advised. He sat down wearing the right pair of glasses waiting for his moment of relax. The timer was fixed for two hours and it switched on as soon as it recognised Andrea's vocal command. The start of the programme was always sudden but the brain as well as all the senses got used to the machine stimuli straightaway so as to enable total absorption by the user in the surrounding environment re-created by the microchip. Andrea opened his eyes to a light azure blue horizon in the distance where the sky and the sea meet. The sun shone brilliantly, so intensely that the golden sand sparkled, the warm wind of the Mexican Gulf blew softly over the skin causing a shiver of pleasure and enjoyment. In the distance the echo of a samba could be heard, mixed with the calls of the seagulls and the sound of the waves which lapped up over the soft shore with fragrances of salt water and the multi colours of the seaside, green, blue, yellow, red…. The calm ecstasy of total enjoyment, peace, not as a simple vacant sense of satisfaction but of a well-balanced life full of energy at rest and balanced. A substantial and perfect peace. The microchip had given and at the same time received the right amount of data to fill the body and spirit. Andrea felt invigorated and outside himself. Suddenly, out of the blue at the climax of the rite, a laugh echoed through the silent bay, a horrible deep laugh which made Andrea so cross that he lost that state of peace and stability he had just found. Quickly the tropical background began to break up and lose its perfect shape turning into a mass of indefinite pixels. Afterwards the colours lost their intensity showing a gloomy sky, more grey-like and dead vegetation showing no sign of artificial life that the microchip had given it. The whole scene started to melt, even the rhythm of the samba had disappeared and now he could hear only the beat of his heart. Terror filled his face as he thought of an imminent short circuit, and so he didn't wait a second more before shouting the command 'exit'. The screen went off immediately leaving a green spray in front of his eyes. Return to the real world was terrible. Andrea's eyes stung and they took a while before they readapted to the lights in the Relax room. Next to him was Alberoni laughing as he leant against the deck chair showing an expression which could be described as a scoff. Andrea didn't intend to react, he had come out of that darkness feeling sick and now under the blinding electric light he appeared weak with little physical strength, no equilibrium and a most agonizing mind.

'Hey, look who's here! Do you plan to run away this time too, Mr. Rossi?' said Alberoni in a sarcastic tone.

Andrea looked at him a second time then waited until his head was ready to come back down to the ground, to reality.

'Stop it, Alberoni.' replied Andrea in a dull tone 'There's just been an accident with this machine. Hardly relaxation!'

'An accident? What happened?!' asked Alberoni with his usual worried tone. Andrea was no longer interested in his colleague's real feelings. After the incident he was too upset to wonder about it.

'The computer went berserk. The programme didn't work properly and caused deformations everywhere.'

'Are you sure?'

'Of course I'm sure!'

'Let me see.'

Alberoni carried out the same procedure: he inserted his E-id, put on his glasses and set off for the Tropics. His holiday lasted a quarter of an hour and he came out of it intact, feeling at peace and as happy as a lark. Andrea rubbed his eyes in disbelief seeing his rite end without any hitches and felt jealous for that peace and stability he had failed to obtain. Andrea was only left with agony.

'Nothing out of order. It works perfectly.' said Alberoni taking the glasses off.

'Impossible.' replied Andrea. 'I saw the sky and the beach melt away just like ice.'

'Andrea, what's the matter? First this story about the psychologist then your strange behaviour... is there something you want to tell me? You can talk about anything to your old friend Alberoni!'

The word 'friend' felt uncomfortable considering the type of relationship that existed between Andrea and Alberoni. The first didn't really care much about the other except for when a petty matter or two cropped up at work or when they met up in town. The other, from the first day they had met at the Fichampon, had always come forward and invited Andrea to join in every kind of activity he did. Nowadays a friend was simply a companion of adventure, someone you spent free time with chatting on very casual terms, nothing deep. In other words, a kind of quick antidote against solitude, and Andrea definitely needed company but that annoying crowd and the stickiness of Alberoni convinced him it was better to be alone with his problem that devoured him. Only his friendship with Marco was different: sometimes right and other times strange, sometimes simple and at times complicated, but Andrea felt fine just the same because he didn't feel constant irritation or uncertainties. It was a special friendship that had helped Andrea understand himself, even if not always in a clear and distinct manner. One of the main purposes of a friend is to bear (in a light and symbolic way) the defeats that we would like to inflict on our enemies. It seemed though, as if Andrea was the only one who had enemies; all the others were cheerful and carefree and didn't suspect their companions of adventure. In this case Andrea couldn't help feeling excluded from the social order even if everyone had overcome every kind of discrimination by now. Indeed, Alberoni had every right to know what Andrea's problem was but not the truth.

'Today I went to work,' Andrea began to tell his story. 'And I received yet another comment from the Manager.'

'Another one?!' shouted Alberoni incredulous. 'It's the twenty-second one you've had!'

'Twentieth' Andrea corrected him.

'I'm not bothered if it's the twenty-second or twentieth, I want to know if you're alright!'

'But yes, of course I'm ok. It's just that I often find myself staring into space. It happens especially at work when I'm writing documents and then soon after I hear the thunderous voice of the master.'

'Mmm...' muttered Alberoni. 'I think you need to have some fun.'

'You're joking, seeing that I can't even use this damn thing?' nagged Andrea pointing his finger at the virtual relax machine.

'I'm not talking about virtual fun, I mean real fun. On Saturday I'm going to a party near Piazza Babila. Why don't you come along?'

Andrea didn't really agree to ending up among the crowds, especially if they were strangers, but the idea to put aside this madness that was persecuting him persuaded him to accept and this time it was he who said a definite 'yes'.

'Yes, maybe you're right. A party is a good idea. I will confirm Friday afternoon, ok?'

'Very good!' exclaimed Alberoni with his usual big white grin. 'See you Friday then.'
Andrea nodded as he thought about the incident with the virtual relax machine; he felt more isolated now than, more isolated due to his desire which hadn't been satisfied, due to his dead satiety. He felt a lot more isolated, more by himself than he had ever been before in his lifetime. Maybe it wasn't the machine's fault, perhaps it was fault of his own, but at that moment in time his thoughts were focused on Alberoni's laugh alone.

Andrea left the CRS at about four something in the afternoon. The turquoise sky was ready to leave room for the evening and from behind the big buildings around Piazza Duomo, the sun reflected its last pale rays over the golden clouds. The usual crowd of people ran backward and forward and according to Andrea's tired eyes he was sure he saw the unmistakable and uniform icon #2744 go by. He suddenly remembered he had to go and buy the new WAP Coloured Hologram 1600 but he couldn't be bothered. He really didn't feel like doing anything so he decided to make his way home. The empty *transport* and streets worsened how isolated he felt. This was the time of day when everyone made their way to the city centre but Andrea was the only one going in the opposite direction; folk were shopping, buying, selling, working, and enjoying themselves and not many were on their way home where an artificial silence awaited in front of the noisy computer screen. Up to now Andrea had preferred to avoid the crowds but now he found himself looking forward to the day of the party to get in amongst the crowd he detested so much, anything that would get rid of that horrible spectre of solitude.

His return home was silent, passing through semi deserted streets, empty stairways, accompanied only by the sound of the *transport* and the voices of three or four people. Room 221b was silent too. Andrea entered slowly so as not to spoil that silence. He didn't even put the light on; he just fell on his unmade bed and looked up at the ceiling trying to relax after his busy day. He was about to shut his eyes, he stretched his legs and glanced out of the window at a point where he could just see a small strip of sky. There, among the clouds, almost hidden by the veil of night, he could just about see the rays of greenish light coming from the Duomo. That's incredible. This was the first time he had ever noticed the light; perhaps it had always been there and he had never noticed it before simply because he didn't usually have the time to stop.

III

That night Andrea had a dream. A strange, very short dream which apparently didn't seem to have any logical sense. He dreamed of a room made entirely of wood which had a table in the middle and on it was a clayish concoction which turned on a strange device. Andrea had never seen anything like it and hadn't even ever seen a wooden hut. In Milan you only saw enormous apartments, all made of concrete and all built according to the Masbuild style which guaranteed every comfort for every month of the year. The latest digital devices were available for everyone. The end of oil, what nonsense! To the contrary, he thought, progress had to be thanked for not forcing us to live in wooden huts like in this dream. He felt the cold blowing through him, his body freezing and the dream seemed so real that Andrea couldn't believe it, he couldn't believe that people once lived in such ignoble conditions. Once. The dream continued. Andrea moved closer to the table where the device continued to go round aimlessly slopping the clay here and there. He felt he wanted to stop that damn machine in endless movement, to bring it to a halt, and he did it by grabbing that clayish mass he had never seen before. It was a new sensation, his fingers ran through the soft surface of clay, re -awaking his sense of touch; a sensation which could be compared to the sensation he had in the Relax room but with a slightly different intensity due to the cold wind which blew down his spine. Andrea shivered. Indeed the mass began to take on a shape, slowly changing shape every second and Andrea's eyes shone with enthusiasm as he eagerly wanted to continue to make a shape and give it a definite form and feel a sense of skill in his fingers. The dream stopped suddenly, it disappeared into thin air just as he was about to push his fingers into the material again. Andrea opened his sleepy eyes and saw it was half past three in the morning on his windup clock. It was another five and a half hours before the alarm would go off and Andrea no longer felt like sleeping. He got out of bed and looked round in the dark. Luckily the candle was still on the desk so it was easy to find to light up. The little flame quivered slightly over the open pages of the diary and shone onto the empty vacant pages. A few drops of wax fell onto the desk, but Andrea wasn't bothered as he was staring at the diary, spellbound by that useless block of paper that according to the old man was a way out. What way out? Andrea sat down and took the pen still lying between the pages. He tried not to think about anything else and concentrated on what he did the day before and his dream, thinking there must have been some connection. Although his eyes were stinging out of lack of sleep he started to write as if he was driven by that same force that had led him to shape that inorganic mass of clay in his dream.

Letter II – Milan 8th November 2073
Today is Wednesday.

Andrea read the sentence. He had tried to copy the letters he had learnt to write as a child on his electronic board at the orphanage, the ones he saw every day in the streets, on his *dvd-screen* or his *digital-desktop*. Despite his wobbly writing, Andrea was satisfied with the end result and carried on writing ignoring the pain in his hand.

It's early morning and I've just had a dream. I dreamt a wooden house, cold and unwelcoming. Inside here was a table with a strange rotating device on it and a pink-coloured clay. I touched the stuff and shaped it with my own hands. I'm excited about what I dreamt even if I don't understand the reason.

Andrea stopped to read over what he had written and was pleased that he had been able to get down his thoughts onto paper, what he felt deep inside. It had seemed difficult and complicated at first but a couple of sentences were enough to convey what Andrea felt; they were there all on the page, hidden between the lines, mixed with the letters in a muddy mass that only required a movement of the hand to make the indefinite, definite. Andrea felt he had made progress, a step toward the unknown that had let him forget for a short moment his physical and mental pain; it was then that he thought again about the old man, a figure that was from such a far off past and yet still so near. He decided he would go and see him to ask for some explanations; he was willing to take another step and get to the bottom of the matter, whatever it took. He never thought he could possibly come across 'a storm' like the one he had been through over the last few days.

In the meantime the sweet movement of the flame made the shadows waver and seem alive in that static silence of the room. Even shadows reigned outside and seemed to fill the empty world of the Darkening.

Next morning the alarm clock went off at nine a.m. Andrea was lying with his arm over the desk and his head on the diary. The pen had rolled down off the desk and the candle was still alight but only a quarter of red wax remained. According to the timed programme, the lights came on a few minutes later and room 221b came back to light after a lethargic night. Andrea could have altered the clock timing to suit himself the night before but seeing as his day looked interesting he didn't want to waste time. The old man would probably not remember him but a visit to his crypt was necessary. Andrea got up from the desk after stretching and opened the wardrobe on the left.

The choice was limited; he had been so taken up with his thoughts lately that he hadn't had time to update his wardrobe. He took off his synthetic deer jacket and put on a blue jumper over his white shirt. He could have got the Decreaser out to give his shirt a fresh look but he didn't bother. He couldn't keep still, he was so excited and couldn't wait to fulfil this scope, this step toward the unknown. He didn't bother eating, nor cleaning his teeth, he was only thinking of going out and his mind was already outside running quickly like an Autumn wind, directed toward the future, toward the meeting with the old man without worrying about the tall buildings in his way or all the streets built by man or the barriers of the external world. The clock said it was quarter past nine. Andrea was already on a *transport* toward Piazza Agostino. The ride lasted almost twenty minutes; the time necessary for a *transport* to get to the centre from the Segrate district. Years ago it would have been impossible; Andrea had read that once Segrate was considered to be on the outskirts and it was impossible to reach the city centre through roads and crossroads blocked by traffic. Eventually the problem was solved and with it all the problems of pollution and accidents. Nowadays the *transport* took everyone to the city centre passing every half hour and thanks to their magnetic system gas emissions were practically a thing of the past. All the streets in Milan were laid with metallic cables through which the electro-magnetic waves passed like sparks dancing to the rhythm of *technoplus* music. Besides, Segrate was no longer on the outskirts because outskirts didn't exist anymore; there was the city centre with lots of twenty storey apartment blocks around it which faded into the horizon beyond Bresso, beyond Rho. The Milanese population had reached ridiculous levels after the Maxi-urbanization of the Global Corp. of the Thirties and housing problems were solved effectively. Thanks to

Global Corp.'s organisation satisfactory results were achieved and the Masbuild style was adopted; it was an idea which came out of the blue to house lots of people in good living properties. However, with the passing of time, birth control and family planning had been considered to create a better balance.

The ride ended in the square which the week before had seen Andrea caught unprepared for the Darkening. Thinking about it now he shivered and could only consider himself mad for putting himself in such danger. He remembered the ambush by the Men of the Night, the arrival of the police, the mad dash for the street cleaner machine and he thought over all that happened that night as it was still so vivid in his mind. Step after step he reached the entrance of the alley way which in the light of day had a different look to it. The morning sun peeped out at a point between the apartment blocks and sent a weak ray of light to the cold metal of the street cleaning machine. Then Andrea recognised a sign but not the usual pop-up message which came up on a computer, nor the usual flashing sign on a *dvd-screen* in Piazza Duomo; it was something more, something interesting and different than the strips of light of the *iperco-ops*, something stimulating Andrea's curiosity, something which made him run down the road. The clock struck half past nine when Andrea took his first big, small step away from the main street. The hole was there about a hundred metres away, just as he had come across it in the dark, hidden by a couple of bricks and a cover that strangely enough had not been there the week before. Andrea moved everything out of his way and slid down calmly as he already knew the way. Obviously the stairway was not in the dark now, a spiral of light penetrated between the bricks and the hole cover but not enough to light the tunnel which was lit by hundreds of candles leading to the old man's room. Everything was exactly like it was before but somehow different as if the brick sequence along the side walls had changed creating a new combination. Andrea felt a moment of fear but he plucked up enough courage to enter a second time into this room forgotten by the world.

The old man was sitting there on his yellowish-green chair with his fingertips joined rather like a web in a mirror, his eyes closed behind his glasses, behind greasy lenses worn out over time. Andrea coughed to make himself noticed and woke the old man from his half asleep state. His eyes were red and tired, also worn out over time but they moved upward to observe the visitor who had come to disturb him. Long, deep wrinkles traced their way along his eyelids leaving just a strip of sagging skin, having forgotten that old previous vital energy. The old man looked Andrea up and down, from head to foot, but he knew who he was.

'You have disturbed me, young man.' said the old man clearing his voice.

'Disturbed?' asked Andrea embarrassed. 'Were you asleep by chance?'

'Asleep?' smiled the old man. 'I haven't slept for years. I'm always awake thinking while stuck in this old cubby-hole.'

'Thinking?'

Andrea was surprised by the word 'thinking', which right from the first encounter had appeared loads of times from every dark and remote corner of his mind. A lot of questions came to mind, hitting his mind furiously but not even a single word came out of from his mouth.

'Yes, thinking' exclaimed the old man noting the surprised expression on Andrea's face. 'Thinking is the best intellectual capacity man has and it is what you have lost.'

Andrea understood that the 'you' was meant for him as well as all the people in the so-called external world. The way he spoke made Andrea go dumb suddenly, such a direct scolding went through him like an arrow. Andrea tried to answer him but not even a sound came out to contrast the croaky voice of the old man.

'You look lost, young man.' commented the old man getting up out of his chair. 'Just like the first time you came here.'

'You remember me then?' asked Andrea amazed. 'That was over a week ago!'

'Surprised, eh?' said the old man dragging his feet toward the other side of the room. 'You didn't expect that from a poor chap like me.'

'Well...I...really' muttered Andrea. 'I didn't mean to say that.'

'I know, young man, I know you didn't want to say that, I know you well enough.'

'I don't understand that!' interrupted Andrea staying on the threshold. 'How come you trusted me from the very first day when I came here? How could you be so sure that I wouldn't have crossed you for any reason in the world? And then why did you give me that diary?'

Andrea finished his round of questions with a serious look on his face but inside he let out a cry of joy, so pleased to have managed to partly express his queries. The old man had his back to him with his hands resting on the desk, the short journey from the armchair had exhausted him and Andrea could hear him panting in the silence. He needed a moment before he was able to reply.

'Well young man,' started the old man. 'I trusted you right from the very beginning, from the very first moment you put your foot inside here. I read in your eyes how anxiety afflicts you, I saw how you are lost, lost in a world which does not reflect your ideals, and lost in something you don't even know what.'

The man had turned around now and was looking at him in the eyes. Andrea was overcome with joy, happy to have got a reply to his hundreds of questions which had been blocking his way forward to happiness for such a long time now. The old man sat down like a dead weight on a stool, still out of breath. Andrea stood still while his mind jumped from here to there continuously, anxious to hear more, to know as much as possible. That curiosity wriggled its way through his body just like the poison from a snake bite which stays there forever.

'You're perfectly right.' said Andrea. 'That's exactly how I feel, but I can't …. I just can't bring myself to say it out loud.'

'Don't worry young man.' said the old man taking on a sympathetic and friendly tone. 'Would you like something to drink?'

He opened a drawer and pulled two glasses and a bottle and placed them on the table.

'Unfortunately, I only have this one bottle of red wine but I think it will do the trick and get rid of our inhibitions.'

The old man grinned again showing all of his yellow teeth as he pulled out a stool from under the desk. Andrea hesitated first before stepping forward to have a look at the bottle but he was surprised to see it didn't have a label. He wasn't sure whether he should drink that wine; it wasn't the usual decisive, dark red colour wine has, but something a bit lighter with violet and purple hues. Andrea felt on edge as per usual, dithering and unsure about what to do. He hadn't trusted his old friend Alberoni nor had he felt free to talk to Marco, so why should he blindly trust this 'granddad' who had come out of nowhere and shown him a dusty diary and a bottle also covered in dust? The jump in the dark was made as soon as he had swallowed the liquor which went down burning his dry throat. It was a simple action which drowned his rational mind and opened up the voice of his conscience, of his soul, the real voice of a man with all his weaknesses.

'There must be something behind all this.' said Andrea after drinking. 'I turn up here out of the blue, in the middle of the night and what do you do?...You hand me a diary without saying a word, no precautions or warnings. You had no idea who I was, you didn't know me; how did you know how I felt?'

'It's true I don't know you.' replied the old man swallowing all in one go the rest of the wine. 'But it's also true that we are of the same kind, you and I. A move was enough, a glance into your eyes and I got the sensation that you aren't at all at ease. Our eyes are the mirrors of our conscience, dear boy!'

'Conscience? Sensations? Tell me, are you a psychologist or something?'

'Not at all, I'm simply a man, a man of the world who has travelled the roads and seen all sorts of people.'

'I'm a man too.' Andrea pointed out.

'No, you aren't, young man.' replied the old man raising his voice a bit. 'You aren't a man. You are just a copy that came out wrongly, an ugly and corrupt copy of my species.'

'What you're saying doesn't make sense!' said Andrea getting up from the table.

'Why doesn't it make sense?' asked the old man in a defiant tone using what little voice he had left.

'Because a few moments ago you said we were of the same kind, then you talk of me being an ugly copy that's come out badly... What you're saying doesn't help one bit, they are just words in the wind. Maybe I shouldn't have come here!'

Andrea was confused, he couldn't grasp what the old man meant even though he was fascinated by the words that flowed out of his mouth. It was the same kind of language with a slightly different touch, slightly stronger, more decisive, but at the same time more delicate. He was sure that in this old cubby-hole lay the answers he needed and he had to let himself go in order to get them. The challenging tone of the old man seemed like a scolding, an arrow through the heart. Maybe he wasn't wrong to have gone there after all, maybe he just had to be patient, very patient. He decided to follow his heart seeing as his mind had become overwhelmed with alcoholic spirit.

'I've changed my mind, I'll stay here.'

The sentence was almost automatic like the click of a switch or the click of the Internet Café keys, like the clicks that had gone on and off after he had spoken to Mr. Vazzano.

'Well,' said the old man satisfied. 'I was sure again that you wouldn't have wandered off from here.'

Andrea stared at him in his eyes then looked down not having enough courage to see the face of truth and reason. He was right, damn it, he was so right. He passed his glass from one hand to another wondering what roads sweet wine can lead one to, especially to someone who had been teetotal from birth.

'This is strong stuff.' continued Andrea emptying is glass with a large sip.

He intended to get back into the conversation at any point.

'Quite strong, I admit.' answered the old man. 'It's been lying under here for at least forty years and if it wasn't for its light colour it could be defined as a vintage brandy.'

Andrea was about to spit out what he had just swallowed.

'Forty years!' he shouted amazed. 'You mean you have been here for forty years, here alone and you have managed to survive?'

Andrea couldn't believe it, not only for the length of time but also for the conditions he and the wine had lived in.

'Yeah, I can hardly believe it myself even now. I came here after 2034. The roads were chaotic after the Maxi-urbanization and it was easy to find this old crypt. It belonged to the Church of St. Ambrogio. Have you ever visited it?'

Andrea was lost again because he didn't want to admit that the old man knew far more than him. He realised how much detail he had left out but he envied him just the same because he had lived the past and remembered the course of events perfectly. Andrea, on the other hand, had got lost in the fog, in a time where the memory got confused and the past didn't seem much different from the present. It came as another scolding, another invisible arrow and Andrea could only give in. In the meantime, he remembered St. Ambrogio's church that he knew very little about; the first thing that came to mind was the nearby market. The concept of church was more complex; his knowledge in this field was limited to notions of 'a place of worship dating back to many centuries ago'. It was a true paradox because all the Milanese people, including Andrea, passed by this fine example every day and it was indeed the best example in existence.

'I came across this crypt,' continued the old man. 'Four walls that had survived the fall of concrete which had covered the old building. I was lucky so I didn't waste my chance and brought as many of my belongings as I could here, leaving my past life behind in the hands of the uprisings of the time."

'And you've managed to get by?'

'Begging and borrowing here and there…'

'Incredible! You did all this and refused the invitation to go to the *gerial*?'

Andrea asked this question as he remembered that in the Years of Change all the elderly were taken to the *gerials*. The exodus had included even people over forty and who knows maybe in that mass of people there was his mother who was a stranger to him anyway, a complete stranger escaping from her past. Gradually after ten years that exodus finally ended, the age limit was re-established at sixty and there were no more problems nor complaints, only the joy of being able to go and live in a peaceful place far from the chaos. This old man in front of him had chosen the opposite; he had denied himself a happy life in exchange for a miserable crypt and four bottles of rubbish wine. It didn't make sense but Andrea preferred not to say anything for fear of being scolded by the old man again. He drank another glass in silence.

'What stupid villages they are!' exclaimed the old man disgusted. 'Nothing more than a cursed devilry of the outside world!'

Andrea grasped the words 'outside world'; the old man used them a lot with an expression of hate and anger as if they were taking his last strength. It was an attitude which took to Andrea indirectly, a silent contagion under the skin, under the grey matter of his rational mind. Immediately the worried face of Alberoni, the damp weeping eyes of Marco, the absent expression of the CEO and the thousands of faces in the crowd in Piazza Duomo came to mind. A man could smile and be a villain, could smile and be happy, just enough to cast a veil of suspicion and uncertainty in Andrea's eyes.

'Young man, are you still there?' interrupted the old man, breaking the flow of faces in Andrea's mind.

It flowed like one of those lists on the *digital-desktop* at work which left Andrea spellbound in a day dream gaze into emptiness, that damn gaze into space.

'Eh?' said Andrea trying to appear present and attentive to the discussion.

'Stop pretending. I saw how you were lost in your thoughts.'

'Lost in my thoughts?' repeated Andrea without really understanding. 'Sorry but I...'

'Why sorry?'

The old man's exclamation surprised Andrea yet again.

'There's no need to apologise when you are only a stone's throw away from the right direction.'

'The right direction...' muttered Andrea.

If what he was following was the right road why was it that the rest of the world thought it right to follow a completely different road? These were parallel roads which Andrea was jumping between, first one, then the other, playing around with other people's words and gestures. The wine started to pinch at his throat but Andrea decided to stop on any road with some company and have his third glass of wine.

'"No-one stops to think anymore".' continued Andrea. 'Is this what you mean?'

'You're different from the others.' said the old man looking straight into his eyes. 'Have you ever thought about that?'

Andrea rubbed his eyes. Those same words, the ones written in the diary two nights ago. Was it a purely casual coincidence? The old man certainly knew a lot of stuff about him, about the outside world; it was all vague but at the same time clear, a gruelling dualism for poor Andrea to bear. The wine pinched at his tongue tickling his drunken mind and empty stomach but there was still reason. Even with a small dose of alcohol in his veins that authentic reasoning remained to annoy and disturb him. Andrea didn't want to quote the words from his diary even if he was on friendly terms with the old man. Well yes it was him who gave him the diary in the first place but the matter of friendship wasn't altogether clear. He couldn't confess such an important secret to him in such a simple manner; people were teased and made fun of for less than that - for an action considered out of place according to the natural state of things. Perhaps the old man wasn't like the others as he had lost contact with the outside world for over forty years but he still wasn't sure whether to open up and tell him everything. This suspicion held back the key which could open the door to his mind but for the moment he would let the old man talk waiting to see what he revealed.

'An explanation. This is what I expect.' said Andrea inciting the old man to speak. Forty years in total solitude. Surely the old man had a deep desire to talk and Andrea was anxious to learn the meaning of a mysterious sentence.

'"No-one stops to think anymore".' repeated the old man solemnly. 'If you are different from them, it means you do stop and think.'

Andrea frowned. The old man had explained it in such a manner it left Andrea perplexed and confused over the word 'think'. He did not dare ask and he was afraid to come forward if not until the right moment. In the meantime the old man's breath began to smell sickly of wine after his third glass. That wine was probably the only real company he had had in all those years, a reason for Andrea to keep away from the stuff.

'Let's forget about the story of my life and carry on with our previous conversation' said the old man noticing Andrea's worried face. 'Biologically we are two men but there is a subtle difference.'

Andrea continued to not understand.

'Biologically speaking us men are bound to the species of apes, right?'

Andrea nodded as he tried to remember all he knew about apes. Once or twice he had been to the zoo in Milan, the one in the centre of the Public Gardens where a lot of animals were looked after in their habitat for the joy of all children. It was spring. He passed by the cages, walking among the balloons and trees in bloom and he vaguely remembered a creature two metres tall with a thick dark fur. 'African Gorilla', it said on the label, and in the meantime Andrea made a mental profile of its physiognomy together with other labels connected to the name 'Darwin' and the concept of 'evolution' that he had once read about in his *ekletto-encyclopaedia* which he had kept separate as if they were a different topics.

'Could you tell me the difference?'

The old man's conclusion plummeted on him once again, unexpectedly. Andrea was busy thinking but he managed to give him an answer.

'Reason, or rather intelligence, ability to use logic, elaborate data…'

Andrea quickly listed some points to show the old man he was no ignorant person but behind that machine-like rhythm he knew he hadn't actually fully grasped the real meaning of his answer.

'Yes, well said, but doesn't anything come to mind comparing the first and second case?"

'That is, as if I were the man and the others were gorillas?'

Andrea reflected for a while trying to find a notion which linked perfectly to what he had said. The answer lit up like a light bulb in a dark room, like a new star after years of darkness in the night sky and nothing stopped Andrea from keeping his lips sealed. He spoke up right away without checking his answer, without connecting words to rational thought, without worrying about the old man's corrections.

'The others are animals without a brain!'

'That's right! You've got it!' the old man congratulated him by sipping some more wine. 'Your answer is more or less right and not surprising for someone who comes from the external world.'

The compliment made Andrea feel happy which turned the dry wine into a sweet syrup. So Andrea felt like asking a question.

'Why do you call me "someone from the outside world"?'

'Do you really want to know? Tell me then, does your life satisfy you? Tell me if you're happy with yourself and what you have.'

The question was direct and it immediately opened a gap before Andrea's eyes, a grey empty gap beaten by a sad wind full of worry. The image seemed real, a pain in the heart and shaking all over his body, and then cold, cold as if the wind had just stirred up and pulled at his clothes. The pale sun eclipsed forever but behind the corner was a new dawn just about to be born; a new stronger sun, brighter and set to spread light every corner of the world. Andrea died and was re-born in an instant.

'Why do you say all these things?' asked Andrea after a moment's silence.

'Hard words like marble, harsh words that bruise the heart…'

Sadness appeared on the old man's long face and changed him so much that he became almost unrecognisable.

'Just don't think about it and you'll be happy!' exclaimed Andrea to soften things.

'I'd rather be unhappy than have that kind of false lying smile that you show.'

The old man's voice was solemn now.

'Well, it was said and done; those hard words like marble have hurt you at the heart and you'll get a scar, an indelible scar which will never disappear! It will always be there, always.'

Always.

Andrea heard the word echo, shaking him. However, he wasn't in a state of shock, he was just more aware about what had happened and what was about to happen. He remembered a similar episode, which emerged out of nowhere, a past event when he was still a little boy, a happy boy who ran carefree along the white corridors of the orphanage. After lunch he used to run and slide along the smooth, shiny floor of black and white tiles, an innocent pastime for a five year old child. White rays of sunshine filtered through the dormitory doors on each side, everything shone of cleanliness and smelt of the freshness of a spring day. It was a day like any other, maybe it was the same day as the visit to the zoo, with the only difference that now he was a friendly child and not the indifferent adult he thought he was. Memories overlapped one after the other without respecting any order or flow of time and something new always came out which had nothing to do with the past or his original memories of his life. And Andrea ran and slid and laughed, then there was a wrong doing and he turned into a melancholic adult. He overdid it; he ran and he swerved on the end corridor and bumped into a woman wearing a white overall. The young woman glared at him and told him off saying he was a mother's mistake and cursing the day she had decided to bring up young orphaned children. Indeed the number of orphaned children had increased greatly at the end of the Thirties as it was a period of crisis when couples didn't know whether to have a natural or artificial child.

Andrea had never known that he was an orphan but when he found out, it gave him a different light on things which set him on a different road, a parallel road which he had always followed unknowingly. It was probably this tiny incident that had changed things for Andrea and in all these years his behaviour had been guided by this event. It had touched him deeply. He had shared night and day with his enigmatic malaise and only now had an answer sprung up out of the river of memories which were streaming out in that instant. Yet again it had all happened with gestures and words, only a few words standing still on two chairs at some invisible point in the world. Andrea spoke breaking the silence and in a way he was sorry he broke the spell because he had never actually heard absolute silence, he was always interrupted by people chatting or simply the intermittent buzz of an electronic device.

'My memory...' muttered Andrea. 'Now I remember...'

'Your memory has always been inside your head and it has never moved from there.' said the old man.

That moment of tension was over and the old man was pleased with the way things had gone. You could read it in his eyes but Andrea was busy reading himself and didn't see the sparkle in his small unlit eyes. Andrea's thoughtful eyes looking down in search of something he couldn't find. Actually it wasn't his memory he was looking for but the world's past, which was marked there in the pavement, in the arabesques of the tiles with their dark gloomy colours, in the dust of times gone by. The desire to know, to excavate down into the foundations of that crypt was stronger than he was and the old man was his only chance since everything he had learnt during his life has suddenly collapsed like the foundations of a house built on sand.

'How old are you?' asked Andrea lifting up his head.

'More or less, I'd say about ninety. Ah, my memory isn't what it used to be. I'm getting really old, young man...'

The old man felt the weight of his age on his weak bony shoulders.

'Your memory preserves almost a century of changes, you've lived those moments and no-one better than you can narrate them.'

'But I don't remember every single moment of my life perfectly!

'Even if I read and re-read as much as I can, I can't get at the information I need nor hold and remember it for more than ten years. You are the only person who can tell me if the world has always been like this as I know it.'

So strong was Andrea's thirst to know, to grasp the flow of time and go forward without looking back that Andrea didn't know whether to shout or throw himself to the ground and implore.

'History isn't just a pure piece of information.' the old man warned him.

'Maybe history isn't that but knowledge is' replied Andrea. 'Knowledge is information and it is important for man to accumulate as much of it as possible to widen his own knowledge. "You are what you know". This is the motto in the *ekletto-encyclopaedia*.'

Strangely Andrea's quote sounded automatic. It hadn't been the first time he had repeated this opening phrase of the *ekletto-encyclopaedia* but his time it sounded different, or rather, it sounded empty and inefficient.

'*Ekletto-encyclopaedia*? Oh yes! That useless multi - media encyclopaedia! I had no idea it was still in circulation.'

The old man's comment surprised Andrea a lot since from childhood he had seen the *ekletto-encyclopaedia* as a valid source of definite knowledge. Unfortunately, the meeting with the old man had also destroyed this cornerstone which left Andrea having to start from scratch and recover that strength he had when he was small, when he spent hours on end in the orphanage library, absorbing data and names which got lost in the wind; data and names which, however, remained in the *ekletto-encyclopaedia* but with the passing of time they became fragmentary pieces of news without any sense.

'But...' Andrea tried to contradict.

'Don't be presumptuous, young man!' the old man scolded. 'You're impatient to say something without having reflected first. Listen to what others have to say and not only the President of that damn Global Corp. or the Pope.'

Andrea let the second name slip without comment and he was extremely surprised by his criticism of the Global Corp. Such a criticism of the great worldwide organization was unacceptable but he decided not to speak up so as not to irritate the old man any further.

'Our brain,' continued the old man 'Isn't capable of holding a large amount of data. Too much information causes an overload or better broadens the mind destroying all wisdom.'

The old man's chit chat took on colour, fascinating Andrea to the point that it blocked any chance of him contradicting.

'The fundamental thing nowadays is information, information without criticism and without any ideas. All those online libraries, all those useless *ekletto-encyclopaedias*, are all a result of television and Internet, instruments which reproduce to the letter all our multi-form civilization in a couple of lines. We should be more selective in our information; get rid of the insignificant and choose what is original and creative. Human intellect is important for this reason and has to work in such a way that the wealth of hardware doesn't replace fantasy.'

Andrea could hardly follow the old man's words. He analysed every single element and recognised the forerunner to the *dvd-screen*, the process of overloading and the concept of multi-form civilization but he couldn't put the pieces of the puzzle together and link them with fantasy.

For all he knew fantasy was 'an imaginative power of the soul and rather whimsical' as the *ekletto-encyclopaedia* stated and it certainly did not mention the old man's discourse. Fantasy was a 'whimsical desire of the soul' and therefore something frivolous which had nothing to do with Internet and human intellect. What did that old man want to imply, a man so old that he no longer had the strength in his arms and yet so young he could talk with the liveliness of a twelve year old?

'I can see I've lost you again boy.' exclaimed the old man interrupting his talk. 'I bet you can't tell exactly what I mean by all this senseless stuff, can you?'

Andrea gave a false smile. The whole discourse seemed really quite senseless but he was surprised to find the old man saying it himself. His answer would have had more effect without a doubt, well almost!

'Fantasy as an imaginative power of the soul with particularly whimsical desires.' said Andrea repeating the definition in the *ekletto-encyclopaedia*.

'That wasn't the question, be more precise!'

Total darkness for Andrea!

'You haven't understood anything at all, young man!' sneered the old man. 'You think you know but it is only an illusion!'

The final laugh made Andrea slightly nervous. He hated to be teased as if he were ignorant. On the other hand the old man was right and Andrea was aware of it. Inside him, he was boiling with anger and he wanted to get away, to get free like a blaze of fire but he couldn't because he hadn't the courage to react and admit his mental void. And so he stood still in a pitiful state of living penance feeling the bitter, torturing truth as it pierced through him two or three times.

'More precise?' muttered Andrea.

'Precision and detail are essential partners in a discussion which allow us to have more in depth knowledge and not a miserable shallowness like the one you just showed.'

'But I replied quickly and concisely!'

'You can answer in a nanosecond or in just a word but the result will always be second rate and incomplete.

Quantity isn't important but the quality of what you say because your intellectual ability depends on it.'

'You mean my culture?'

'No, culture is theory. I'm talking about practical things.'

'Manual work and suchlike I imagine.'

'Not at all. I'm talking about mental work, or rather creativity.'

'And where is all this written?' asked Andrea curiously.

'Wait a moment..."' answered the old man with a satisfied air.

He got up from the chair placing yet another glass of wine on the desk and he went toward a large cupboard on his right. The four wooden shelves inside it creaked under the weight of the thick volumes of books and from one of the rows the old man took out a large dusty book. Hundreds of sheets of paper slipped out and fell onto the carpet; they were yellow with age and they became history right away making space for new pages.

'Here it is.' said then old man. 'This is one of the true sources of knowledge.'

He threw the heavy book onto the desk and lifted up a cloud of dust over Andrea's head. There was the title written on golden characters on the front cover although it was hardly readable. It read '"The Divine Comedy" by Dante Alighieri'.

'I know this book.' said Andrea. 'I happened to read a review about it a few years ago.'

'Review? Bah!' said the old man indignant. 'It's better if you actually read the work itself if you don't want to offend the literature of your country.'

Andrea turned red for what he had said; he certainly didn't want to be disrespectful but he didn't understand why all these sheets of paper were so precious to the old man.

'Read and reflect boy!' said the old man as he opened the old volume. 'Read and reflect without speaking!'

Andrea obeyed and saw the title printed in black on the first page, then on the next page there were the first lines and so he began to read in silence.

Midway upon the journey of our life
I found myself within a forest dark,
For the straightforward pathway had been lost...

Surprised, Andrea stopped reading. The form and elegance of those words had little sense to him but the sound and rhythm of the verse matched his state of soul and made him feel well, freeing his mind and heart. It was as if he no longer needed his body, as if something from inside was trying to break out and declare itself free, out of the walls of flesh and bone. It was as if he were on the top of a mountain looking down at the dark abyss of ignorance and the harsh obtuseness of the rocks. He would have liked to ask a question at that moment but the old man wanted him to reflect first before speaking. He didn't know what to do so he carried on reading.

Ah me! how hard a thing it is to say
What was this forest savage, rough, and stern,
Which in the very thought renews the fear.

So bitter is it, death is little more;
But of the good to treat, which there I found,
Speak will I of the other things I saw there.

I cannot well repeat how there I entered,
So full was I of slumber at the moment
In which I had abandoned the true way.

At that point Andrea felt he had to say something after feeling that majestic sensation of serenity that those words instilled in him. It was exactly like those MIDI tracks that followed the right sequence pattern, a parallel path between his wave length and that magic text which ended in harmonious and unmistakable melody. Andrea lifted his eyes from the page and saw the old man blissfully sipping another drop of wine. Neither of them really remembered how many glasses had been drunk but there was already another bottle of sweet nectar on the table waiting to be poured. Both by now were really out of the real world, out of space and time, where past and future coincide in the mitigated present.

'How was this person able to write such wonderful words?'

'He must have been upset or deeply hurt inside,' answered the old man. 'Otherwise it's impossible to create sentences that are so true and penetrating like an X-ray.'

'Sadness...' whispered Andrea. 'Harsh words like marble, harsh words that scar the heart.'

His eyes looked for the old man's hoping to find a sign of approval, but he had turned his look to the bottle and with the same sad face of before he had changed the topic of conversation too.

'Well then. Do you understand the meaning of this poem?'

'Not really...'

'I see, it isn't simple stuff like those silly texts for the Opsolector! Wait while I read you another piece and then my message will be clearer.'

The old man turned over the page and began to read aloud. The tone was different now, more authoritative, more articulated than it seemed, as if it was he who was guiding the flow of words and not the mute and motionless book. His talking reached its climax of splendour and clarity and became music to Andrea's ears, just like a MIDI track, only that it was a bit more real.

And even as he, who, with distressful breath,
Forth issued from the sea upon the shore,
Turns to the water perilous and gazes;

So did my soul, that still was fleeing onward,
Turn itself back to re-behold the pass
Which never yet a living person left.

'These verses,' said the old man as soon as he had finished reading aloud. "They are more than seven hundred years old and they still have the same glory that has made them important even today…?'

The old man saddened for a moment and Andrea saw that glory in the light of his tired eyes, a light that had once twinkled with extreme intensity. Andrea wondered if he would be like him one day and at the thought of it he shivered. Indeed, at this point what would have changed in his life after everything that the old man had told him? Would everything remain the same? Would fresh air have taken on a different fragrance? Would his days have been brighter? Or would he have lost all of it? It cast a doubt on his existence so he thought it was better to get back to the original topic of the book before every kind of sadness overtook him but the damage had already been done. Anyway, was he sure it was damage, or maybe it was something positive?

'What has this got to do with creativity?' Andrea asked.

'The author has created an atmosphere which hasn't to be intended on a purely real level. The words he uses are metaphors and the fact they are written in an old, Italian language enrich the structure even more. A metaphor as you know is…'

'I know what a metaphor is!' said Andrea remembering the electronic course on digitalization he had done. 'But I can't see any link with my cultural problems.'

Andrea couldn't fathom what the old man intended but some ideas were floating in his head even if they weren't clear ideas.

'Today everything is created by machines in a very generic way and the result is the *ekletto-encyclopaedia*. This man here however invented and created making use of his own skills; he wrote over a hundred 'canti' using his head! The only thing you can derive from this is that he has a special mind that makes him different from all the others. I am different from you as I said before.'

'Only in the mind?'

'I'll give you a more modern example: see this bottle of wine? It hasn't got a label on it and it looks unusual. I bet you again that if you go into one of these..... *iperco-op*s, you will never find, absolutely never, a bottle like this one. Try and maybe the concept of particularity will become clearer.'

Andrea at this point would have preferred to return to the original magical text of this medieval poet but he stored the information just the same tempted to try and find out later what the surprise at the *iperco-op* would be.

'So this...erm...Dante, what did he mean by these words?'

'Simple, his poem is the memory of a journey beyond the grave, whose experience is to be an example to all humanity lost by their mistakes. It is a psychological relation between past experience and moral conquest of the present which lets him be judge of himself and all humanity, and be poet and main character in his poem.'

The old man finished his speech with a deep sigh. Ever since he had pulled out his thick book he had been over excited just like a young school boy, absorbed by the

desire to convey his knowledge; in the meantime Andrea
sat there fascinated and thoughtful, a habit he was
beginning to relish.

'Internet has never told me all this. So it's true then,
it's a bit of a joke. You're right when you say it's
useless.'

'Not exactly. Once the Net used to be one of the few
resources people had to be able to talk in absolute
freedom and break the unnerving consistency of
widespread information. It was a way to see a fast object
as it flew low, invisible to the big media companies'
radar, but with endless excuses and powers of all kinds
they tried to enclose the Net and reduce it to a controlled
channel of mass culture, so consistent and repetitive that it
had lost all its flavour. Naturally they were helped by the
immense power of that frightening destructive force that
continues to afflict our species: stupidity. Perhaps they
haven't completely managed in their quest but soon the
grip will tighten even more…'

I'm losing track of our conversation again, thought
Andrea trying to grasp the line the old man was taking.
Up until a moment ago they spoke of memory and
knowledge without Internet while now he was defending
the Net and accusing the so called 'powers' which Andrea
had never actually heard of. Being closed up in that place
for so many years had led the old man's desire to talk to
someone to the limit of the impossible and he had started
to talk freely, endlessly, without stopping. At first Andrea
doubted him considering him a bit mad, but now that he
was so deeply involved he had no other choice but to
follow his tone way road to its very end.

'Internet has undergone numerous changes since optic
technologies came into being as they have led to the
passage of millions of bits a second. The nucleus of the
Net has stayed optic but extensions use a whole lot of
other technologies to be able to get access and Internet

has spread on an interplanetary level covering all earth's surface with its databases. Is there by chance a negative side in a society flooded with information and the tools it makes use of to run it? Enormous quantities of data are about our private matters, and the decisions we make, which flow through Internet with the intention of improving our lives. Despite our inclination to give up our privacy in exchange for convenience, our experience on line make us yearn for the anonymity of the past.'

Andrea was terrified by the old man's spirited eyes who in the meantime has got up with his hands pointing to some vague point in the ceiling. Was he delirious? Andrea didn't really know how to react; it was dangerous to interrupt the old man in such a delicate situation. Listen, he said to himself, listen.

'Who is able to filter such a vast amount of accumulated information without leaving a trace of personal cookies spread all over the Net?' continued the old man. 'How can you be sure that the information at hand for everyone has not been altered in some way from one day to the next? How can intellectual property be protected?'

The old man looked down toward Andrea as if to stress how his last few words had made more sense than the rest of his discourse. There was a moment of quick glances at each other, as quick as a sunbeam of the morning sun which springs up suddenly behind the Milan apartments, as intense as the strong taste of the wine on the table. Andrea saw the light of the truth and at the same time the flame of anger that he had already experienced with Marco's reaction. Who knows if he and his parents had the same relationship with the past and with that life style which was so new to him; another doubt, only another doubt to add to the long chain of uncertainties.

'I believe I have finally grasped the meaning of everything you are telling me" answered Andrea a bit uncertain. 'I have to use my head to see what makes it different from the uniform masses, right?'

'Clever boy!" exclaimed the old man quite thrilled.

A quite singular character, thought Andrea feeling proud of the compliment he had paid him, a great man with a past and all its adventures. To tell the truth he knew very little but his life did seem to have been very fascinating.

'Could I borrow "The Divine Comedy"?'

'No.' warned the old man. 'My knowledge on paper must not leave these premises. It's dangerous.'

'Why?' asked Andrea amazed by the old man's protective attitude when a moment before he had announced himself the disseminator of real culture.

'For two good reasons, boy.' answered the old man pointing his finger at him. 'First, I don't want to see this copy at risk of being swallowed up by the outside world. Second, if you really want to be creative, it's better if you use your own head without use of any external sources. I've shown you the way, it's up to you to follow it.'

The explanation was clear and Andrea felt he had not to insist, not to contradict what were absolute priorities for the old man. According to him, it was not right to limit another person's will, but for the people of the outside world what the next person felt was of no importance.

'Well then, I think it's about time I left.' said Andrea getting up from his chair.

The effect of the wine made him sway a bit but he was able to stand up.

'Alright boy, I don't want to keep you any longer. But please remember to reflect!'

Andrea nodded with a smile, giving that same understanding look he had exchanged with the old man two weeks before. Without saying another word they both knew they had something in common, an inner spirit that let them be on the same wavelength, but Andrea's rational mind was now absorbing the alcohol again and it hadn't fully accepted this new teaching. He began to feel the confusion between the external world and St. Ambrogio's crypt.

The old man said no more and went back to his armchair. Andrea wanted to say goodbye properly and thank him but he didn't feel up to facing this mysterious and exceptional character who couldn't be described in plain, simple words. There was an immeasurable strength inside that man, capable of moving saggy muscles and strengthening decalcified bones. Andrea wondered if Dante would have been capable of describing the soul of this old man, then another doubt crossed his mind. Just then he remembered the challenge of the *iperco-op* and his rush to get some light on the bet with the old man made him leave in total silence for a second time. There were so many other questions to be asked but the old man had decided to break off any discussion for the moment and Andrea had agreed, although the old man's last words like 'privacy' and 'protection' and 'power' made Andrea curious to know more.

While the old man went back to his thoughts, sinking into his rickety armchair, Andrea was already outside under the starry sky of Milan. Time had flown in a flash from nine in the morning to early evening, Andrea couldn't believe his eyes. There was no clock whatsoever in that hole as far as he could remember, no reference to present time. Maybe he hadn't taken notice so all he could do now was guess; however, the strangest thing was that no biological or mechanical sign had reminded him of a specific duty of the day: food! Only now did his stomach start rumbling, tired after so much wine which had dried his throat and left his body drunk; hunger took priority and Andrea put all the day's events in the back of his mind. All he could think about was rushing to the *iperco-op* in Piazza Duomo, the vital lymph of the city.

The clock on one of the entrances of McDonald-Nestlé's said it was seventeen forty five. That constant flow of people on the stairs and in the corridors of the *iperco-ops* at every hour of the day made him think of static time that always stayed the same. Seconds passed quickly, so quickly that he couldn't count how much time he had wasted; on the other hand, in this day and age there were no longer any binding deadlines or rather, even if there were, they didn't have to be done straightaway or it was nothing that your life depended on. However, for Andrea there was something that needed immediate attention: check that bottle. Andrea had suddenly forgotten how hungry and thirsty he was, he was so involved in that alienating eloquence in the world of his obsessed mind and now it was priority to find out what the old man's message was. He chose the first supermarket he came to and began roaming the aisles among the shelves full of packets and jars. The impact was almost immediate, as soon as he had finished roaming the alcohol section; there wasn't one bottle identical to that extravagant one, maybe something slightly similar but not the same. The light of truth shone again on a detail, on a deficiency in the mechanism which Andrea had considered perfection from the start. In the search of the bottle, Dante's mind revealed its unique potential in the usual routine of everyday life and Andrea could do no more than run away, not being able to stand the old man's prophecy, which without a doubt was totally true. Outside the misty shop windows on the first floor, the wind had struck up, blowing the coloured posters and twisting musical slogans. Andrea liked the autumn breeze, it made him feel light-headed, but that busy city bustle brought on an anxiousness and he didn't know why.

IV

Vazzano's apartment was located in a more central position compared to Segrate, and given that the *transports* that day were in reserve that day, Andrea had to get there directly from home either on foot or even on his Monopad. The morning had passed quickly: wakeup call at eleven, some *dvd-screen*, a bite to eat. He had slept well compared to previous nights and from this point of view he envisaged a better day. However, toward midday, he suddenly felt hungrier than he had done the night before and since he hadn't eaten anything for over twelve hours, the only thing left to do was run to the Remote Control Express point, press the right pads and chose something to his taste. It was a special kind of service which connected you to the McDonald-Nestlé so you could order any kind of ready meal or frozen food or it even connected you to another *iperco-op* which sold every kind of purchase. By using the electronic shopping service you could do your shopping without moving from home, thanks to the efficiency of robotics. Indeed all the apartments within the urban network of Milan were wrapped around transporter belts, metallic conductors and robots which forwarded every possible thing. In less than half an hour the McDonald-Nestlé switchboard sent you a portion of fish and chips, and finally Andrea sat at his desk in front of a hot dish and ate hungrily. In the meantime, the weather was being shown on the *dvd-screen*, announcing calm weather for the whole day. A jingle in the background accompanied the geographic map of Italy with its display of clouds and suns. Next to his plate was his diary, but Andrea didn't consider opening it, he just looked at it with each mouthful, thinking about the old man and his words. It wasn't the right moment to start writing, the only thing to do was meet up with the old man again after his visit to the psychologist. He sat looking at the *dvd-screen* until one forty, zapping between some news and *rapop* music then at about two he took out his Monopad and set off on his long ride toward Vazzano's office.

It was two forty-five on the landing clock when Andrea was invited into the room to start the sitting. Mr. Vazzano was waiting for him impatiently on his swivel chair whilst he tapped his fingers on his *digital-desktop* which clearly showed the name 'Andrea' written in bold. What good timing by the CEO, thought Andrea! He had already informed and recommended the psychologist to notice any flaw in his condition and the latter was ready to give him confirmation if necessary. Following night's council, Andrea had reflected greatly on recent events and had decided to conceal once and for all his real feelings toward the external world. In this way he would have avoided the bad looks from the CEO, Alberoni and also his work colleagues; it was a way to calm the waters so he could concentrate more on the old man. He had never lied in his whole life, not that he had ever needed to, but it was the right time to change, to turn over a new leaf. He calmly sat down on the Plexiglas chair and waited for the confrontation.

'Good morning, Mr. Rossi,' said Vazzano breaking the silence. 'And welcome to my home-office. I have been informed about your work break and I preferred to call you here in person rather than have a virtual interview. Indeed I mean to talk to you seriously. The CEO of the Compagnia states he has had to intervene and carefully consider your case of absent-mindedness.'

'Absent-mindedness?' muttered Andrea with fake amazement.

'Yes.' continued Vazzano ignoring the deceit. 'This is the result coming from our Knowledgeer. You know about this, don't you?'

'But of course!' answered Andrea openly. 'But I didn't think it was such a serious matter. Look, I'm already better and ready to start back at work again with commitment and devotion.'

The words came out on their own, masked but spontaneous, full of persuasion and astuteness: a gradual change in Andrea's behaviour.

'I'm not so sure at this point.'

'Well, why don't you wait for the next check up by the Knowledgeer and you will have confirmation.'

'If you really insist, Mr. Rossi. But I believe you should fill in these forms.'

Mr. Vazzano pressed a button and the image on the *digital-desktop* came up in Andrea's direction so he could read it. It was a plain white card with questions on it, multiple choice and some blank fields. Andrea smiled with cheek and took the keyboard in hand.

'With pleasure!' he said.

The sitting was short. It lasted about an hour without many complications. Vazzano didn't notice anything unusual and left Andrea feeling quite calm. The questions were easy, aiming at understanding his personality through a mathematical point system with a final pass mark, and Andrea knew how to get round that, also because he wasn't ill, he didn't have any mental illness; his rational mind was always the same while something else continually changed which didn't have anything to do with letters or numbers.

'How's your cold?' asked Andrea handing in the test.

'A thing of the past.' answered Vazzano glancing at Andrea's answers. 'Yesterday I went to a genes programmer and I was completely immunised. I advise you to have it done so you will finally be able to say good bye to every kind of cold! Besides, it could also do something for all your white hair, I don't know why you don't do something about it.'

'I will do something.' exclaimed Andrea smiling.

Vazzano was right. Ever since that first white hair had appeared he had never thought of taking advantage of the modern biotechnologies. There was time, but it was running out while he was deciding about what to do; the world now let you change your physical appearance but Andrea was destined to change inside.

'One last thing.' said Vazzano. 'Could you please give me your E-id? I have to load a few personal note for the Company.'

'Orders, Captain!' joked Andrea.

His fake behaviour was sinking into the ridiculous in order to ingratiate himself with the psychologist, especially with those false big smiles, big as Piazza Duomo. He gave him his E-id card and Vazzano inserted it into the drive behind him. The following data appeared on the screen of the *digital-desktop*:

<u>Name and Surname:</u> Rossi, Andrea
<u>D.O.B. (Date of Birth):</u> 24/04/2038
<u>D.O.S (Date of Systemship):</u> 02/05/2059
<u>Profession:</u> data miner

Under the first data set there was a list of civil and juridical notes written by Global Corp. as well as other stuff. Mr. Vazzano entered something into the work section but Andrea couldn't read what he was writing.

'I see you started your career a year after your twentieth birthday.' commented the psychologist when he had finished writing.

'I know.' said Andrea losing some of his smile. 'I asked to be included in the GASA in 2058 to take part in space missions but as I was the last candidate I was preceded by others. Then, I took part in a virtual Master course in Turin to enter into the scientific field but I didn't get in again. In the end after a year of various attempts I became a *data-miner*.'

'Well, I imagine you enjoy working for the Compagnia.'

'Without doubt. I love being the main support column in a perfect system.'

The lie had all its fascination and Andrea knew he could use it as his protection shield. His job wasn't such a great thing he thought it was and after eighteen years he had finally considered   having to break that fake perfect system; without a sound he would have broken it to see what kind of circuits there were inside it.

At about four o'clock in the afternoon, Andrea left Vazzano's study with an expression of content; another step forward had provided a huge relief. The streets were still empty with just the odd person here and there, some were on foot, others on their speedy Monopads. The blue sky had turned grey with clouds, quite the opposite of what the forecast had foreseen and he could even hear some thunder in the distance, but only a light rumble not at all threatening. Andrea rode freely on his Monopad toward Piazza Duomo and for the first time he decided not to stop there, in the absolute centre of Milan. He thought of all the busy traffic, especially the cars; it was after the first alarm of the energy crisis that Global Corp had decided to abolish cars, and as far back as Andrea could go, it must have been about 2044 when he watched for the last time, one of the last racing car rallies. Even today he had never forgotten that event and in particular that red car which came into the room; it had a large black horse on a printed yellow background on its rear boot. How strange it must have been to be able to drive along the roads with such freedom! Andrea sighed. The world of cars was in the past now and had absolutely nothing to do with his life. He imagined a Milan crowded everywhere and not in just one place; his Monopad passed quickly by the crowded *iperco-ops*, through the empty world of tomorrow and he pushed on further, in the opposite direction to the vile, furious masses, toward the crypt of St. Ambrogio where among the columns and bricks the past was hidden. The old man was there as usual, sitting in his armchair, waiting for him, and this time he had a dusty, rusty classical guitar in his hand. The six chords played sweetly with the light plucking of the old man's numb and wrinkly fingers.

'Twelfth Meteo!' interrupted Andrea recognising the jingle of the weather forecast. 'I don't know how you do it but you manage to get a perfect melody.'

The old man lifted his eyes up but he didn't look too pleased nor surprised but rather a bit annoyed by Andrea's unwelcome comment.

'This is "Yesterday", you donkey!' warned the old man. 'Don't offend the music of past times!'

Andrea felt a bit embarrassed and happy at the same time, maybe because he had gone back to that place where a scolding meant more than it was worth. Contact with every single word spoken by the old man, whether a scolding or a compliment, put him at ease.

'This is the conversation we had yesterday.' answered the old man keeping a serious tone. 'The vast information media alter reality but it seems as if you haven't grasped this concept well enough.'

'I have understood the concept of creativity and detail.' reacted Andrea. 'However, you haven't given me any explanation about the "vast information media". What on earth are privacy and protection? What are the "powers" you keep talking about? You haven't told me anything about them!'

'I've already told you, boy.' answered the old man keeping calm in front of Andrea's rude reaction. 'Unfortunately I can't explain everything, you have to use your head a bit. This song is part of the past. It's a masterpiece by the Beatles. Don't you understand? Comparing this song to that jingle means altering reality and transmitting wrong information. The signature tune for "Twelfth Meteo" isn't original, it's a fake.'

'The past gets lost in the fog even in this sense?'

'See, you can get there on your own!' exclaimed the old man pleased. 'When your mind begins to work it opens up your eyes on everything forever.'

'It's true.' said Andrea seeing the light. 'Excuse me, I didn't want to appear too instinctive.'

'Don't be silly, boy" the old man encouraged him. 'Man is instinctive by nature, it isn't something you have to feel guilty about". The old man's tone was still calm bearing no sign of nastiness or sarcasm. Andrea admired this old man because of the relationship he had created with him out of nothing; it was a relaxed and pleasant relationship but above all innovative in his ordinary life.

'Come on, don't just stand there at the door as per usual. Come in! I heard the thunder and it's going to pour down very soon. Take a seat here.'

The old man pointed to a pile of dirty white cushions lying next to him and then got up to put his instrument in the old cupboard. This simple action of getting up lifted an annoying veil of dust into the air which fell back onto the cushions and around the room. Andrea needed a genes programmer or a tissue engineer to treat his delicate nose, but as per usual he hadn't had the time to see about it. He sneezed twice. His eyes were red and swollen but he decided to put up with it as long as he was warm and comfortable.

'Do you suffer the cold?' asked Andrea remembering the genetic operation he had had a year ago. 'Haven't you ever thought of going to the Policlinic Hospital like I did? Biogenetics does wonders these days.'

'Reaction too uniform for my liking, just like information.' answered the old man indifferently. His back was turned, his body in the dark and his face looking down at his desk. The flames were dancing on the wax columns placed all around the room and in the silence he could hear wine being poured into glasses accompanied with a gentle sound of rain falling which had begun to wet the streets and roofs of the buildings.

'Wine, books and music.' commented Andrea rubbing his chin. 'I thought you didn't have any pastimes.'

'Thinking is a pastime.' said the old man coming back carrying two glasses of red wine. 'I think it's sufficient. Here, take it. It'll keep you warm.'

'How can you say thinking is enough?' asked Andrea taking the glass between his two hands.

'There's too much free time, son. We are full to the brim of forced time fillers and our minds are in overload.'

Andrea linked the word to the discussion of the day before and he got ready to concentrate on the theme of the latest conversation.

'We worry too much about what to do.' continued the old man in his usual eloquent style. 'The fear and uselessness of a void imply a need to schedule something.'

'And what would the point be of standing still, staring into space and doing nothing?' responded Andrea thinking he had made his point. 'I think it's a waste of time!'

'Waste of time…waste of time… What do you mean "waste time"? Time and the importance of things can be so variable. Letting your mind drift into reflection in an empty world doesn't mean you're doing nothing but that you're using your inner eye and not the outer ones. Wasn't it Pascal who said that man's troubles come from his inability to sit still alone in a room? Perhaps you haven't realised but your mind is free now!'

'My mind is free and relaxed when I'm at the CRS…'

'…under the effect of virtual reality!' concluded the old man a bit ironic.

'How do you know?"

'I know a lot of things, boy, more than you can ever imagine!'

'Are you trying to tell me something about the CRS that I don't know?' asked Andrea imagining some kind of uncovered mystery. The old man continued to surprise him; his modernity contrasted with his ties to the far off past, his perfect knowledge of the external world even if he lived in this cubby-hole; it all left some doubt about the story of his life like a chain whose rings didn't match up perfectly.

'You must know that centuries ago, I'm talking about a long time before you were born, the Industrial Revolution brought about a ruthless social struggle to have machines. In the twentieth century the steam machine was turned into a computer into bits and data running on silicone microchips. At the CRS you see hundreds of electronic brains that do nothing more than stimulate your brain cells with impulses, reducing you to something worse than a vegetable. Information society is nothing more than isolation from perceptive reality. Every time we are in front of a computer screen and we have a one way conversation, it's always man who suffers. You programme and manage the computer with ease but he doesn't answer you and you become dependent waiting for an answer.'

'And all this paper?' Andrea refuted pointing to a pile of scattered sheets around them. 'Paper in books doesn't answer to you either. Virtual glasses at least let you live real emotions in first person.'

'This is true.' answered the old man approving. 'But a book, instead of damaging, it stimulates your fantasy and in this way man can find a way to a satisfying world of dreams.'

'Look, the world of dreams isn't touchable with your hand!'

'And neither are the fake scenes created by a processor! They are dreams invented by someone else; so how can you be sure they correspond to your own desires, your fantasies?'

The question, just like all the others, put Andrea in a situation a bit like checkmate, when you look in vain to find a way out, a solution, and at the end you give in coming to the conclusion that your opponent has won. Andrea detested the fact that he couldn't solve the problem there and then but he was aware that the incident of two days ago at the CRS justified everything the old man had said. The crashing of pixels, the loss of colour; they weren't a play on the mind, it was an unconscious reaction by his mind which refused the electronic impulses. His inner eye saw only grey, grey everywhere, even in the autumn bronze sun, and it was a sign showing what his enigmatic problem was. It was important though to understand the reason for all this, the true value of this route that had carried him far off, perhaps too far and beyond. The dream about the vase came into Andrea's mind and he tried to imagine its meaning but couldn't come up with anything. He didn't want to ask the old man as it was a personal matter.

'A machine has some difficulty to interpret fully human feelings.' added the old man in conclusion and Andrea was given the final confirmation. 'Use your inner eye and you'll see your conscience will guide you and enable you to see what letters and numbers can't explain.'

Just like in Vazzano's case! Andrea suddenly lit up and remembered the test and how easy it had been to cheat. The same thing at the CRS, the same man-machine relationship. Andrea smiled.

'Getting back to free time.' said Andrea. 'Why don't we mention those pastimes that don't involve any electronics? For example, the sports fields at the Public Gardens, tennis there requires a certain ability without any help of hardware.'

'You're right, but first I told you that too much free time of any kind occupies the mind and therefore your argument fails.'

'And what do you say about travelling? Going away as far as the Canary Islands every month is a dream that becomes reality and difficult to say no to.'

Andrea felt the weight of his words on his heart, as he had just refused a similar trip. What an idiot!

'Here we can move onto another topic: holidays. You may define them as relaxing, exciting, or the height of pleasure even if people continue to go to the same destination.'

'Well, what do you mean by that?'

'The big global world guarantees a hundred per cent fun but if you want to come across even better bargains it means discovering another kind of hell.'

'It's absurd to call hell an exotic place, like the Canary Islands or the Caribbean.'

'Well, when you discover the world of fun you live in is just the same, you realise that it is more than correct. They are all the same, the same identical things everywhere. Unfortunately, those days when the risks of adventure were a pure dose of adrenalin are over, when the unknown was a real source of emotion.'

'But aren't you pleased man has managed to explore all of our planet? Thanks to sophisticated GPS satellites that revolve twenty four hours a day we manage to see every dark remote corner of the planet.'

'And once that last dark corner has been discovered, good bye to its uniqueness which makes it so special. Have you ever thought of going to an alternative destination?'

Andrea thought for a moment. Every part of the planet had its own tourist area; the Caribbean for the Americas, Madagascar for Africa, The Indonesian Archipelago for Asia and in each case that same holiday village was on offer with its prefabricated bungalows, its swimming pools by the sea and multi coloured cocktails. It was possible to leave the village to visit pre- arranged places. You could go wherever you wanted, even to Easter Island, but the same things were on offer just maybe in a slightly different setting. Andrea realised what the old man was getting at but he still wasn't satisfied with his explanation.

'Europe offers an excellent service to the Canaries or the Balearics.' answered Andrea. 'Anyway, if I were to choose a far off place I like, I would choose the Maldives, a holiday destination between Asia and Africa.'

'They're too far away!' moaned the old man. 'Why do you want to go so far away? Can't you find somewhere just as exotic but a bit nearer home?'

'You mean like Sardinia?'

'Not only. For example, why don't you choose a small island in South Italy called Capri? Once it was the glory of this country, the flower in their button hole...'

'Times have changed!' interrupted Andrea decisively. 'All the Italian coast, islands included, disappeared after the De-glaciation period.'

Andrea had a sudden flashback to the news now available on his *ekletto-encyclopaedia*. The De-glaciation period was a phenomenon in parallel to the energy crisis, it had been going on for tens of years without anyone's concern. The melting of the polar ice caps had taken place very slowly so only after years and years had they swallowed up and drowned forever most of the land's surface. Climate change and the changing of the coastlines had led to Maxi-urbanisation all over the world, there was a mass migration flow towards the metropolises to be safe from the ecosystem's radical changes across the planet. The *ekletto-encyclopaedia*'s explanation ended here, but Andrea wanted to know more, to go beyond the boundaries, get out of Milan and see the cliffs that were once the green hills of unknown lands. He really longed to do that but the darkness of an unexplored world scared him and persuaded him to stay safe and sound within the safe invisible walls of Milan. However, he really longed to delve into the past now that he could easily access it without the help of an *ekletto-encyclopaedia*.

'On those submerged ruins,' carried on the old man with the same determined voice. 'The damn Global Corp. built the foundations for a new world and with the new global attraction it has destroyed antique traditions.'

Andrea was surprised yet again by the old man's attitude and felt the need to understand the reason for all his rancour towards Global Corp.

'I insist to know why you hold so much anger toward the great Global Corp.?'

'Who holds all the information? Who produces the *ekletto-encyclopaedia*? Who organizes the global village? Who makes the decisions about work, holidays or pastimes?'

Andrea could only think of one name written on golden letters on each and every product, on every web page, on any object of any kind in this world: Global Corp., the world organization that the whole world saw as their saviour from chaos. However, this unhappy old man didn't think the same way and sighed a wish to go back to the way it was before.

'I see,' said Andrea. "But traditions, what have they got to do with all this?'

'Do I have to give you another example like the bottle?' said the old man in a sarcastic tone. 'Well, did you see that unusual instrument I just put away? That is a typical object coming from Spain. Today, however, countries no longer exist so what remains? Only a string of vague regions where the traditions get mixed up and lost, becoming something superficial and vague, becoming an object without a past nor a future.'

Andrea had put the example of the bottle to one side and had almost forgotten that it was this example that had helped him with his visit to Vazzano. He still wasn't aware though of the doors that were about to open up before his eyes; the light of truth was so blinding that he couldn't make out any clear figures.

'I didn't find the bottle, if that is what you want to know, but why are you attacking the Global Corp. now and talking about traditions?'

'The bottle was a simple example just to explain the concept of detail. My intentions go really much deeper than that. A nation. Do you know what I mean?'

Andrea got his grey matter to start working: he knew that in the past there were a whole lot of independent countries spread all over the world, Spain was one of them, but after the last UN treaty, borders had begun to disappear and the world had become one big conglomeration eliminating every form of local government. This was the result of the great globalization and it was also the dividing line with the chaotic past the old man had referred to before. Andrea began to wonder what the logic was in this suspicious and worrying conversation, it was hard to pinpoint the complex reasoning. The bottle, the instrument, Spain - too much confusion in his head that wouldn't let him concentrate enough, and if his mind hadn't got a clear idea as to where the situation was leading, it was easy to fall into the trap of automatism.

'|Groups of people.' answered Andrea. 'Groups of people that have the same common ethnic origin, the same language and traditions.'

'This is what the *ekletto-encyclopaedia* says. What's your opinion?'

Andrea was in total darkness!

'But don't you see? Ethnic origin, language traditions. What I'm trying to tell you is that Global Corp. stopped all that. Progress had trod on the past, turning it into a vague notion and so we no longer know the exact origin of anything. In this global world there is no space for fragmentary things.'

Andrea was surprised by the old man's words and how he came to explain everything starting from rather insignificant detail. He had made Andrea curious and driven him for once and for all beyond those doors, so near yet so far away, behind which there was a hidden truth that the Global Corp. had cancelled under tons of concrete and steel. Persuasion gave off nectar and honey because the greater a man's talent is, the greater his power to persuade someone.

'The Global Corp is the saviour from chaos.' contested Andrea. 'Global Corp has brought peace and well-being. How can you say Global Corp. is an enemy?'

'Monopoly, my boy, monopoly!' shouted the old man banging his fist down on the arm of his chair. 'The control and power that Global Corp has over the world, over its past and over your life, isn't at all fair; it doesn't let you get any satisfaction out of life!'

'But I am satisfied with my life!' exclaimed Andrea feeling a tremble though in his sentence. 'For instance, Egonomics allow me to organise my work agenda, do it as I like...'

He stopped suddenly and only then he realised his false step, the lie he had told in order to defend himself. What he was saying was not true but he had been used to saying it for years, repeat it until he was convinced his life really was interesting. He saw the old man's I-told-you-so expression but he didn't take it as an offence. Indeed all this talking had helped him open up his mind, to let him understand everything with his own brain and make him aware of his situation. He was finally ready to break the system and open up a gap in the dark and mysterious side of the Global Corp., and the only serious directive came from the astute old man.

'Egonomics' continued the old man as he sipped his wine. 'Lets you do what you want but no-one teaches you how to do something. If you are disoriented, who guides you seeing as you no longer have parents? Global Corp. and its global system. Your development is therefore very generic and full of common place ideas because everyone is brought up and educated the same way. Here's the result, everyone is alike according to Global Corp's regulations.'

Andrea remembered straightaway the detail, the diversity of that alternative way the old man had preached so much plus the fact that he had mentioned his parents which left him speechless. Could his childhood and his education be the cause of his uneasiness which wouldn't allow him to feel comfortable in company? He was different from the others.

'I…' muttered Andrea. 'I have always believed…'

The sentences, the words, things so certain that the whole world population had never thought of doubting them, they no longer made any sense to Andrea. The dissonance was irrevocable, and it was useless to hang onto the last certainties which were slowly slipping away like branches floating on water driven by the strong current.

'You're so used to hearing bullshit they tell you that you never think of contradicting it and end up believing that everything is complicated.'

'I can't believe that everything I do is wrong and doesn't make sense...'

Andrea put his hands over his face as if he were trying to escape from the world for just a moment so he could think. A sharp, pain hit his stomach and he felt as if his whole body was emptying leaving him feeble and defenceless. Then he felt a sharp burning in his eyes and tears began to weep from his tired eyes. His cheeks turned red like flames and the salty drops reached his mouth, making poor Andrea shake and he realised he had reached the climax of his desperation. From a certain point of view he felt ashamed of his behaviour in front of the old man but he couldn't help himself as for quite some time now he had always held back showing no pain when in front of friends, or his boss, or a society incompatible with his own feelings. How could such an old man understand his problems inherent to an external world? A veil of silence fell over the room just for a few seconds, long enough to understand the regret and self-pity in Andrea's covered face, a face that had had enough.

'Making mistakes is only human my friend.'

The old man's tone changed suddenly. Andrea peeped from between his fingers to see the old man put his glass down on the floor and was moving his arm toward him. He shut his eyes tightly out of shame, he was afraid the old man would see his red face, but he didn't. Instead he put his hand on Andrea's right shoulder and as he moved closer he embraced him intensely. Andrea stood still but couldn't help sighing, and staring into the darkness he saw himself as a creature driven and mocked by his vanity, and his eyes continued to burn even more so, out of torment and wrath.

'The seal of so called "freedom" means not being ashamed of oneself. Unfortunately, we have learned to accept our limitations. So, instead of looking at society as something terrible, like a restrictive compromise, we have gracefully come to terms with the conditions of Global Corp. contract. No individual has any freedom within an industrialised, oppressive and impersonalised society; the extreme defeat of man comes when he no longer cares for rebellion, when he loses any hope of freedom induced to a psychological acquiescence.'

The old man spoke solemnly while Andrea listened carefully, more and more fascinated by his chatter worth listening to. Indeed, when a discourse describes a passion, we find the truth of what is being said within ourselves, which we didn't know was already in us so we are led to love those who make us feel it. They didn't highlight their own well-being but ours and so this benefit makes us love them as well as the fact that this shared intelligence we have with them persuades the heart to love them even more. In this case Andrea adored the old man for his paternal way of talking, for his ability to instil confidence in him; he looked at him from his feet upward, the way you would look at a sun you had never seen rising before, like a guide you had never followed, like a father you had never had.

'I've got to go' said Andrea as he moved out of the old man's embrace, not knowing how to react to a similar gesture. He didn't act out of indifference but simply because he wasn't used to this kind of relationship; to tell the truth he had never felt such a strong sensation toward an old, decrepit person he didn't even know. He stood up quickly, dried his eyes, still red and looked around but without crossing the old man's stare. He had quickly got used to the darkness of the crypt so he could easily make out any new features. The room was full of drawers, compartments, niches and alcoves; hundreds of places where books, glasses and various other objects could be stored. The whole room was enhanced with wooden furniture, making it magnificent, royal and grandiose in all its artistic beauty. Andrea couldn't help but compare it to where he lived, in an all-white empty room, with just four pieces of plastic furniture put together and the rest was hidden in a tangle of Internet optic cables, in the plastic of electrical appliances, in the wonderful facilities all microscopically installed. All the Masbuild apartments were built in the same way, just like the offices, where apart from one shelf with vases and statues, there was only a desk supplied with the *digital-desktop*. Andrea was describing something too real, because by observing the emptiness of his room in this way he was underlining the emptiness of his life. Andrea took a deep, sigh and walked toward the exit but before he could disappear the old man pronounced his last words.

'*Memento postridie*, son! Remember tomorrow!'

Andrea turned back and looked at him for a last time and before turning the corner he said a simple but sincere 'thank you'. Outside in the alley drops of rain began to fall heavily like bullets, and as he left the warmth of the crypt, Andrea breathed in the cold fresh November air and didn't think to protect himself from the rain. Rain wasn't an enemy, it was a purifying water passing through his body and soul, divided by an indisputable hate, and erasing every imperfection. His mind would become a *tabula rasa*, a clean slate free from guilt and fears. Forever.

V

That night it took Andrea a long time to get to sleep but as soon as his eyes were shut his brain started to come into action and began to build and model images as if they were real. Andrea found himself inside the wooden house, numb from the cold and in front of him was the same table, the same machine. This time he was sitting with his hands pasted with the mass of clay which had slowly changed shape thanks to Andrea's clever hands and had become a vase or a jug. Every pressure with his fingertips smoothed out the clay surface and with every press with his nails he created original lines and symbols. He enjoyed creating the detail in his decoration. It was gratifying. Unfortunately it didn't last long, rather it was only a short sequence of images but sufficient to convey something to sleeping Andrea's subconscious. The dream disappeared suddenly and Andrea realised he was back in his same old apartment. It was still night and still raining outside but Andrea was pleased with what he had made in his dream. He got up to tell someone about it but in that room at two in the morning there was no-one waiting to listen to him, not even the chat service seemed alive enough to appreciate his deepest feelings.

The next day Andrea met Alberoni half way between his house and the Policlinic Hospital. The *transport*s were still in reserve and the rain had fortunately stopped. It was quite a distance to walk but strolling with Alberoni he didn't feel the fatigue because he was quickly absorbed into a discussion of some kind.

'I'm going to buy myself the new UTMS Esovirtual 2800 in a few days!' exclaimed Alberoni with his usual childish enthusiasm. 'A few days ago I got an ad leaflet in my S-mail and so I decided to buy one. It's a really useful gadget you know?'

'I was thinking of getting the new WAP Coloured Hologram 1600. That must be fantastic too!'

'What on earth are you thinking, Andrea? A WAP isn't so great; it's too cumbersome. The UTMS, on the other hand, fits comfortably in my trouser pocket. What a shame, I thought you'd seen the adverts! It doesn't surprise me so much seeing as your mind is a blank – you're still wearing the same jacket you had on the other day!'

Alberoni shook his head and Andrea looked down at his clothes. The same suede jacket! He had got changed so quickly that he wasn't even aware of any other clothes in his wardrobe: it was proof that in the last few days he hadn't thought of himself nor the world revolving around him. The old man's words continued to echo in his head but he had to be careful to keep a vigil and respectable aspect in the external world if he wanted to continue his game of deceit.

'Too many comments from the Director!' chanted Alberoni in a subtle ironic vein.

'Look, I'm better now!' exclaimed Andrea laughing. 'I feel full of beans!'

Indeed it was true and made more sense than any other cell phone on sale. They continued walking and chatting about various things, about the party coming up tomorrow night, the cloudy weather and then they arrived at their destination.

The Sperm Bank, in the east wing of the Policlinic Hospital, was a specialist ward that worked jointly with the Genome Room, which was an area where the full data mapping regarding the genetic codes was held. The various combinations had been studied in every minute detail thanks to the help of the electronic elaborators and having the fundamental data had favoured the disappearance of all illnesses so that a genetically strong and healthy man could be created just as they had done with plants and animals in the bio-agricultural farms. The final characteristics required for the creation of an individual was then assigned to the Incubator that started work by following the formation and the development of the embryo. The remaining ten floors of the building made up the *pedotrophium* where the Company's children were looked after and brought up according to the rules of Global Corp. to be ready to populate the new world.

The whole assembly chain was enclosed in a complex called Celera Genomics which took up half of the enormous Policlinic; the other half was used for correction work on already developed and grown individuals, or rather every kind of surgery, plastic or genetic, capable of re making a person's body perfect again. Alberoni was born here, passing from ward to ward since birth while Andrea had spent his childhood in the orphanages on the thirteenth and fourteenth floors which no longer existed. The new generation was made up exclusively of children of Global Corp and only a few older people in the various *gerials* could still use the title of parent. Andrea was half way between these two worlds, between the old traditional one and the new progress, not knowing hardly anything about either. Before being able to donate a test tube of sperm to the embryo factory for a second time, the two sat in the waiting room and Andrea took then opportunity to ask Alberoni something about his childhood.

'Allow me to ask you a question, Alberoni.' said Andrea turning toward him. 'What was your childhood like here at the Celera Genomics?'

'My childhood?' said Alberoni taking his eyes off the Opsolector fixed to the desk. 'For what I remember it was a happy one. I remember the group games we used to play, the electronic races, the hypnopaedic nights, lots of happy times, but nothing in particular.'

Andrea saw that Alberoni could remember very little about his childhood, probably one or two events were vaguely imprinted in his mind. If ever Alberoni had taken part in all the activities he mentioned, the probability that he could remember any of them was minimal seeing as his head was full of Global Corp principles. Alberoni led a full life just like any respected child of the Company; he certainly couldn't keep up with Andrea who in the void of his crisis could do nothing but think.

'Now that I remember,' continued Alberoni reading the Opsolector again. 'There were several groups divided according to age, and the didactic activities were organised by the nursing staff. When I was sixteen I was part of the Gamma group and we led a life based on lots of sport and plenty of outings with friends in the group. Then the following year I went into the Delta group, the final phase where every day there was an electronic course to face. Once I had reached sixteen my training was complete and the careers orientation group suggested that I work for the Compagnia. I'm twenty now and proud of my choice.'

Andrea widened his eyes. What kind of pride could you get from a job that was almost imposed on you? He felt anger and soon after sadness, not for Alberoni, but for the Egonomics, which was nothing more than an empty word, an illusion, an instrument to help create predestined roles. Knowing perfectly each and everyone's genetic code, made it possible for Global Corp to share out the various jobs and at the same time keep the citizens under the thumb of the mother society.

'I know why you're asking me all this' said Alberoni suddenly.

Andrea tended his ears as in that precise moment he felt bare.

'Your childhood wasn't a happy one, was it? You're lucky if you lose a parent, and if you lose both is work of pure precision.'

'Who said that?' asked Andrea.

'Oscar Wilde'

'I didn't know you had read Oscar Wilde!'

'In fact I haven't read it. I read the quote on the Opsolector.'

Andrea would have liked to reproach him for his ignorance but he held back. Oscar Wilde was a writer of the past like Dante Alighieri he would never have written such a sentence in harmony with Global Corp.'s creed. The information had surely been manipulated, but there were a lot of things that Alberoni didn't know which he wasn't required to know anyway. When someone asks you why the sky is blue or who created the world, well, whoever are you to answer if you have spent all your life in a closed world protected from many external influence?

In the meantime the nurse had announced their turn and the two of them made their way in, down a long corridor with glass panels on either side. Through these they could see the Incubator number 24 on the floor below where the various genetic engineering plants worked and panted without stopping. The mechanical arms moved in harmony before the eyes of the scientists and they grasped the test tubes, modelled the embryos, reproduced: the great demographic machine procreated with a Ford-like rhythm. Observing the procedure from the glass panels, Andrea limited himself to a comment only on their efficiency but he couldn't resist the idea that man was built and assembled the same way a machine was. Of course, the physical differences among individuals were upheld, but their thoughts, their mentality, had to be approved and there was no escape from this since this birth place held you bonded forever and didn't allow you to live your life the way you wanted.

'Thanks to all this,' said Alberoni pointing at a plastic vase and the scientists. 'We'll give demographic control a hand! It's funny knowing that within these four walls there could be a new CEO or even a new President of Global Corp.!'

'Or even a *data-miner*!' suggested Andrea wishing to underline the job they had in common.

'I see you too are pleased to work here for the Compagnia!'

Rubbish, thought Andrea with his false smile. He couldn't stand certain formal and repetitive set phrases, especially spoken by Alberoni who was just a poor naïve boy unable to break out using his own spontaneity. He was still locked inside his test tube, an invisible tube full of childish and embryonic fixations. Andrea saw his face reflected in the glass panel, and sighing, he couldn't deny the truth: he was an ugly and corrupt copy of man.

That evening Andrea tried to forget the chat at the Sperm Bank trying to concentrate on the updates coming in on his S-mail from the Company. He had to carry out tasks carefully keeping his mind and body separate. There was nothing new, just a few reminders about the current situation. Andrea pressed a few keys aimlessly while he glanced at the computer but the corner of his eye slipped slightly to the right where the red diary lay open on his desk, made bright by the neon light shining on it. It was nineteen twenty p.m., still another forty minutes before the candle took the place of the white light filling the room. Temptation was strong and inside he was dying to write a few important words down. Thinking the time was right, he left his keyboard and moved toward the desk and the white pages, which seemed almost surreal but concrete at the same time like earth and cement. His pen danced delicately over the page following an imaginary line, a line of thought that Andrea was aware he had and was able to use. And although he couldn't actually touch these reflections, the words enriched his spirit and filled him with harmony as they materialised on the pure, plain paper.

Letter III – Milan 10th November 2073

Creative writing is like a large pump which keeps the pressure pleasant and constant and allows us to give vent to every engorgement of the soul.

The soul, eyes within, something that wasn't distinguishable in the Knowledgeer circuit. That metallic, invisibly digital beast in the Cedir stood there still without giving any signs of life. Each one of its responses, made up of bits and data were organised by the man who led the Company in name of Global Corp. That same man who had waited impatiently through the optic fibres of the *dvd-screen* for Andrea's arrival that Saturday morning. The digital hands in the lower right corner of the *dvd-screen* showed nine o'clock a.m. when the young Milanese man came into the large hall at the Fichampon.

'Welcome Mr. Rossi!' hailed the CEO. 'Please take a seat and let's start right away to try and solve the matter once and for all.'

Andrea didn't say a word, he simply nodded and behaved like a willing person would. He sat on the reclinable seat and stared at the metallic point. It was a challenging stare. The machine and the human mind. Andrea shivered inside, a feeling he could invert that flow of electrons and inject his mind into the Knowledgeer's. When the CEO activated the machine, Andrea didn't close his eyes immediately, he waited a moment , the same moment which had demolished in one stroke all of his thoughts and beliefs, the same moment which put him face to face with an infinite void of particles.

The procedure took longer than the first time, and Andrea had to withstand twice the heat the infernal machine was producing non-stop. Then the room reappeared before Andrea's rather dazed eyes. The images were partly blurred and partly clear. Andrea rolled his head round a couple of times and then turned his head toward the *dvd-screen* to hear the CEO's verdict.

'You may go.' said the CEO in a calm and indifferent tone. 'Your level has been restored. I'll see you on Monday, Mr. Rossi.'

He didn't say another word, he remained synthetic and silent as he read the data on his office screen. Such behaviour wasn't so new but Andrea looked at it from a different angle and interpreted it from a new front. The eyes are the only part of the mask to remain uncovered so it was easy to read the multiple reflexes on the bright iris, an imaginary game of mirrors that made you suspicious and wary toward any illusionary effect. Precisely at that moment Andrea saw a reflection and an air of restlessness behind that still and austere face. Unable to see everything, Andrea spread his imagination and penetrated the barrier of the *dvd-screen*. What existed that was so alarming at the end of that invisible tunnel always pointing to the same person? Was it maybe his own imagination playing nasty tricks every time he looked someone in the face or maybe there really was something hidden behind the CEO's cordiality?

'That's the end of the test, Mr. Rossi' said the CEO observing from an angle.

Andrea calmed himself down and exchanged the glance. The exchange left only a vague sensation that both were hiding a secret or nursing a few doubts in an area where no other cybernetic instrument could reach. Andrea was the first to withdraw his glance. The temptation to challenge taught to him by the old man was strong but perhaps it was better to keep calm so as not to be in the eye of things. However, as he was making his way to the exit, he felt the CEO's stare right up until he reached the exit. An unbearable pressure! It would have been better if he had turned round and protested but that wasn't possible since he wasn't in the right shape to do so. When the CEO shouted loudly 'Long Live Global Corp!', Andrea replied accordingly out of duty but in repeating the phrase he was in no way addressing the authorities: his diversity was beginning to take shape.

Before leaving the Fichampon, Andrea popped into the office to have a quick look at his e-mail. He inserted his E-id Card but the server didn't show anything new apart from the old message from Alberoni. There was nothing else, no request from the Company, no warning, no S-mail. His inbox was empty and Andrea smiled at the idea of having a free weekend to look forward to.

Saturday night, the only night of the week when the Darkening was more flexible and was twenty minutes or half an hour or even one or two hours longer. Milan didn't change at all in that lapse of extra time: the stream of people remained constant, the large *dvd-screens* constantly showed their slogans and bright multi-coloured displays and products kept flashing and materialising on screen until they broke up into a cloud of vague images diluting their message. Wasn't the quiet of the Darkening better perhaps? Andrea really believed so and that's why he waited on the less frequented side of Piazza Babila. By this time his almighty colleague was probably in Piazza Duomo toying around and would appear at any moment, but after a short wait he saw him coming from the opposite side to the expected one.

'And where are you coming from?' said Andrea surprised.

'From the Public Gardens.' answered Alberoni. 'I went to see a basketball match with some old friends.'

Alberoni never had a moment's peace, he was always busy doing some kind of activity. And he was always cheerful and snappy.

'What time is the Darkening tonight?' asked Andrea changing the subject.

'Didn't you see the announcement on the flying airship?' exclaimed Alberoni. 'Today they are giving us three hours of light! Great!'

'Interesting!" said Andrea with hardly any enthusiasm. He disliked the idea of having to stand a fair bit of light and the noise of the city for quite some time.

The party was on the top floor of the New Microsoft-Sony Building, but it wasn't far enough from the noisy streets down below. As for the party room, it was bound to be one of the many rooms made available for hire by the *iperco-ops*. They were usually hired out for ordinary parties but Global Corp. never missed an occasion to advertise one of their new initiatives. There was probably the mark of some *venture capitalist* behind the party that night too.

'Who organised the do?' asked Andrea with a mixture of indifference and curiosity.

'A *venture capitalist*' answered Alberoni. 'Someone I have known for many years. He wanted to throw a party to promote one of his new projects.'

'I bet it's going to be a fantastic evening!' Andrea commented using his usual subtle sarcastic vein.

The lift ground to a halt announcing it was at the end of the line and the dialogue between the two suddenly ended with a 'ding'. As the doors opened, Andrea was struck by the size of the room before him. It was immense. Bright and multi-coloured, it shone with the light coming from the halogen lighting which radiated out to its every corner. Long rows of adverts and abstract paintings ran endlessly along the walls as yellow as the sun, while the prefabricated wooden cupboards and fabric settees filled and enhanced the empty spaces. The harmony of the furnishings suggested an air of comfort and serenity accompanied by the soft clinking of champagne glasses and Andrea all of a sudden felt as if he were for a moment back in the old man's house. What spoilt it all was the sight of a crowd of guests mingling amid the furniture as if they didn't really belong in that splendid scene. Out of that same crowd came a man, who with a smile on his lips ran forward to welcome the new arrivals.

'Alberoni!' exclaimed the man with great warmth and affection. 'How nice it is to see you again! I was beginning to think you weren't coming!'

'Giorgio, my dear friend!' said Alberoni shaking his hand. 'How could I possibly miss one of your parties? I'd like to introduce you to Andrea, a colleague of mine from work. Andrea, this is Giorgio Manzetti, the *venture capitalist* I was talking to you about.'

Andrea held out his hand exchanging the same formal smiles of the other two, and clenching his teeth, he damned the day he had accepted this invitation to the party. He was completely out of his familiar environment here which made him feel uneasy especially now that everything seemed so uncertain and changeable. In that world of happy appearances there was no place for truth and Andrea deeply wished he could have been anywhere else but there. After unwillingly shaking hands, the best thing he could have done was disappear by the back door, but Giorgio had already invited them to join the others who were making toasts over and over again, unaware of their real existence. Andrea had no intention of getting lost in useless conversations and stayed there in silence in the back-rows, listening with a meditative expression, reflexive, feeling more and more sensitive toward what the people were whispering around him.

'Us folk from Time would like to know your feelings regard the present situation?' said the American journalist connecting the Streamer to the system. 'Is it true that in the last five years you have reached higher production levels?'

'The *pharmafarmers* are doing an excellent job!' exulted the *ecoscout* proudly. 'Production continues perfectly, what more can be said!'

The man was helping himself to a drink from the bar. He was wearing a dark green velvet suit with a yellow stripe of the Global Ecoscout Association on the pocket.

'This Martini isn't bad at all!' commented the *v-dentist* in a professional tone of expertise. 'Just the right amount of alcohol for our organism.'

'You never stop working, do you doctor?' said the girl standing opposite him, smiling.

'Dear Debora, you really should be aware that medicine is the queen of the world. If today we can live happy ever after, it is thanks to the genetic programme of the Policlinic Hospital. Nature has no more secrets. Word of Life.'

'Working through a screen all day is easy.' commented the young *v-mechanic* sitting on the white sofa. 'I was explaining to one of my clients the other day how to fix an Opsolector. Do you know how long it took me? A quarter of an hour!'

'Really, you're joking?' asked the *beta tester* raising his eyes up from the Opsolector on the black table.

'Not at all. A holographic projection of the system in question is sufficient and the client is more than happy to proceed and follow the instructions online. Even one of the babies of the Alpha group would be able to do it. It's as simple as pie!'

'Statistics show that the bio-agricultural buildings in Milan are the best at the moment.' said the journalist as he pushed grey metallic buttons.

'One last question: does commuting have any effect on you?'

'Commuting no longer exists! I can quietly do my work from home and go into the office once a week. The nice thing is that we all enjoy this privilege, even the *pharmafarmers*!'

The journalist recorded the comments one by one and sent them out immediately in audio and video mode. In the rush to get on with the procedure he seemed as if he believed every single word of the *ecoscout* who peacocked around like the best genetic controller of Brianza.

'Thanks to the SV Monorail I come and go like the wind!' concluded the *ecoscout* with a laugh.

Andrea stared at him for a moment and he remembered the SV Monorail. It was the world's fastest link which connected the cities all over the world, including all the peripheral infrastructures. Andrea had been on it only once to go to Turin but he had soon forgotten what he had experienced. He tried to pretend to be the *ecoscout* for a moment, feel the wind beating against the window, see from above the raised bypass the unspoilt nature and ruins of past times covered in musk and ivy. That area was a stone's throw from his home but neither he nor the other four million nine hundred and ninety nine people had ever had the courage to pass over that invisible wall around Milan.

'I get by and make a living as a nurse at the Celera Genomics. Some time ago I was doing P.E. with a group of Gamma students and it was a real treat. These days youngsters are always so sweet and never a nuisance. And you, doctor? Nothing new to tell me?'

'Well, only the usual. Virtual dental frames are the trendiest thing at the moment especially among the natural children. Poor things! Every time I have to waste kilos of stabiliser to relieve their sudden acute aches and pains. I wonder whoever let them be born to live in such a bad way. Tell them Debora what it means to be a son of the Compagnia!'

The two laughed cheerfully showing their white and perfectly aligned teeth. Andrea looked at perfection straight in the eye and found nothing in his favour.

'How's your research coming along? Are you still working on the same project?'

'Of course, I just finished it the other day. It's a new software for the Entertainment Hall at the CRS and I seriously hope that Mr. Manzetti will approve it. You know I'm an *e-preneur* who never gives up! In your opinion why do you think I came to this party?'

'Long Live Global Corp!" toasted Mr. Manzetti looking out of one of the huge windows.

Andrea was sitting beside him, busy choosing the right drink from the tray and he had the chance to observe him with discretion, squaring him up from head to toe. He was wearing a white jacket with a black shirt. His elegant manners and the cigar in his mouth contributed to giving him that extra something considering the role he had. The *venture capitalists* represented a consistent and homogenous group of knowledgeable people capable of directing in a united and centralised way. Manzetti must have been about Andrea's age maybe a year or so older but his appearance didn't show it. He was a child of the Company, with slick hair, attractive, athletic and perfect. He was a man capable of holding the reins of any situation, perfectly suitable for his pre-defined role. Andrea, on the other hand, was forced to put up with his thirty-five years, greying hair, looking a bit melancholic, being out of shape and absent-minded. Someone or something was telling him something was wrong. Money didn't come into it because that wasn't a problem, privileges didn't come into it either because everyone could enjoy all the same facilities. Work, however, did make a difference. Andrea was a *data-miner* and he would remain one till it was time for him to go to the *gerial*. On the other hand, Manzetti was a *venture capitalist* and had the prestige of being someone with special, well balanced talents, a calm type capable of making his place as a man. This is what troubled Andrea, corrupted by envy and the impossibility to find peace and stability. But if economic and social stability had been achieved, what was really missing? Scorn didn't seem to be a plausible reason to justify his shameful introversion.

'You're right!' said the man by Manzetti. 'Ever since the GASDAQ index has reached the stars we should make a toast to Global Corp every day.'

The casual look really suited him: he was wearing an azure shirt and a yellow tie with a Smile on it. He was an *IPOcounter*, a so-called economist whom received bits and data from every corner of the earth to then send it to the GASDAQ, the electronic system of listed shares. Maybe he was the person Andrea sent his data to? Whom could say? An S-mail only transmitted a message and then it was the task of the satellite to launch it into the pile in a flash. It could end up in Tokyo, Santiago or end up again in Milan; it had no identity, only a myriad if wires passing from one router to another on which Andrea read the exhausting passing of time.

'The data confirms an excellent performance by the city' continued the *IPOcounter*. 'If it wasn't for those boys in the Compagnia we wouldn't have been able to affirm such wealth and wellbeing.'

I'm one of those boys, Andrea wanted to shout but it was senseless to say it because he wasn't the only *data-miner* present at the Fichampon. In teamwork shared among hundreds of people individuality was easily lost but this had its advantages seeing that the data Andrea had sent recently were totally made up from scratch. It was better to keep one's mouth shut. He took a flute of champagne from the tray and decided to change scenery. There was a mega screen in a small adjacent room playing out loud music coming from some music channel. The flow of music and images looked like the flow of running water from a tap, a continuous, non-stop and unbearable flow. The guests were going mad dancing, regardless of anything, they were like demons dancing around a fire. In the utter confusion they would never have listened to what Andrea wanted to say; and so his ego shrunk instantly and he hid away behind his unhappy shadow finding a suitably quiet spot on a solitary balcony.

From there you could just about make out an endless horizon of skyscrapers; on the opposite side you could see the fairy lights of the Blue Moon and the passers-by walking along the transparent corridors of the McDonald-Nestlé building. Up high stars twinkled escaping the laser beams coming from the Duomo, hiding from the flashing lights of the city. Their sparkle dominated the bluish scene and their beauty filled hearts until they were overflowing with joy. Andrea was speechless and took a deep breath as he saw this magnificent spectacle, which was so quiet, so different and far from the artificiality of their modern lives.

'It'd be nice to take a trip to the ISS!' exclaimed a female voice coming from behind him.

The usual repetitive phrase, thought Andrea, a bit annoyed, but when he spun round he couldn't help but react to the beautiful creature who stood before his eyes. The red-haired girl stood there on the threshold of the glass door holding a tropical cocktail in her hand. She was wearing a dark blue suit, a jacket with buttons down the front and a skirt above the knee; the tight fitting suit showed off her perfect shape and Andrea seemed to contemplate the infinite constellations in the sky in that night blue suit.

'I hope I didn't disturb you' continued the girl. 'I saw you here all alone so I thought you might need some company.'

The girl came down the steps walking with such grace and loveliness. Andrea made a nervous giggle and looked back at the view trying not to show any hate toward that beautiful girl who had broken his sacred silence.

'What a fantastic view, eh?' said Andrea winking at the scene above his head.

'Sure!' answered the girl leaning on the rail. 'A nice autumn evening.'

Andrea looked at her and out of the corner of his eye saw her incredible beauty. Her hair fell freely down over her velvety neck, framing the face and highlighting her light blue eyes like two drops of crystal on candid snow. An angel fallen from heaven had come between him and the world and now she was there next to him to eclipse the moon and the stars.

'Pleased to meet you. Laura Panucci.' continued the girl, and as she turned, she showed her white and sexy smile.'

'Pleased to meet you too. Andrea Rossi.' replied Andrea exchanging smiles and keeping calm. 'You're here for the party too?'

'Yes, even if to tell you the truth I was getting a bit bored.'

'Me too. Maybe because I don't know anybody except for the friend I came with. I still haven't figured out what the party is for!'

'A very boring convention. Don't worry we're in the same boat. I haven't been in the Systemship for long so I still have to get acclimatised.'

'How old are you?'

'Twenty one. I started work a year after the set age and you've no idea how many times I tried to get my career started.'

Andrea was struck by her openness, by that personal experience she had suffered, and it automatically made him curious to know more.

'And where do you work now?' asked Andrea.

'I work in the transport sector of the Compagnia' answered Laura. 'I'm responsible for the railways to be more precise.'

'Strange. I've never seen you at the Fichampon.'

'Well no-one hardly ever gets to see me. I've chosen to do tele-work and believe me, there's nothing more comfortable than working from home.'

'Do you like the kind of work you do?'

'It's nothing special.'

Laura's answer seemed sincere, natural and pure. He could see the indifference in her eyes, not the enthusiasm that Alberoni had. He wondered if she too really hated her job, who knows if she too wasn't in harmony with her surrounding world. Andrea wanted to talk, explain things but the desire to hide himself was stronger. Distrust held the key to opening the door to his heart and left him hovering between the external world and the inner one. It took time and meditation to listen to one's mind, while to listen to one's heart it took only an instant. Talking to Laura, Andrea had found a peace he hadn't known before and he realised straightaway that she was special. For this fleeting reason Andrea couldn't help worship her perfection, her fleshy delicate lips, and her long slender legs.

'Listen… Andrea…' said Laura suddenly as she moved nearer to his ear. 'I have been observing you for some time now in the hall.'

Her voice turned into a whisper which he could barely hear, it was a sensual tone which gave Andrea a shiver down his spine.

'How about going to my place to have some fun while there are three hours of light left?' asked Laura straightening her skirt.

Such an indecent proposal came like lightning, and unexpected as it was, it provoked an awakening of Andrea's senses, so much so as to convince him to send everything else to hell just as long as he was happy among others and above all with himself. And so that was how they got to know each other biologically speaking.

Andrea had never been very familiar with love making and his experience was proof that he wasn't such a fantastic lover. His last relationship dated back to the Day of Light during a holiday in Toronto six months earlier, it was a casual affair and a long time ago. Sentimental matters often faded into the background under the weight of everyday life and so it was a relief for Andrea to have a woman by his side under the warm black silk sheets.

Laura's body was like a harp and Andrea's fingers moved over her body as if they were playing the strings. She was there in bed, lying on one side, so straight and slender that Andrea was dying to silently lie down close behind her and take her by the shoulders and whisper something silly and affectionate in her ear. She seemed so fragile that he wanted to defend her and stay alone beside her to protect her without anyone else around. The turbine of passion had been so overwhelming as to bind them together for a fraction of a second, but their encounter was already a thing of the past and Andrea wanted to remember it, keep the soft light of the room and the perfume of his beloved in his mind. Andrea stretched out his arm to light the small bed-side light. The digital clock next to it indicated twenty-two forty-five p.m. and the Darkening had not yet come into place. He got up out of the bed and looked for the bathroom door.

His head ached slightly maybe due to too much champagne while all the rest of his body was still wrapped in the warmth of the covers. Today sex was really easy to get ever since women had been made sterile from birth; only the cult of pleasure remained without any of the worries. It was just then that Andrea thought about test tube babies, about the babies procreated by women using their own fertility; he remained perplexed when faced with the idea of having a child naturally. Having a certain responsibility was a condition completely alien to his way of thinking but alive inside him. As he thought about it he felt empty. A sudden urgency to be alone overcame him and he regretted having got caught up in this mess. He didn't have the time for such sentiments. He wasn't in the right frame of mind to carry on a relationship with Laura. I don't need this, he thought to himself, but looking at the bed he felt the remorse of desire since man could prove both indifference and lust at the same time. Andrea removed his stare. Because he hadn't managed to be alone on the balcony, he now really felt the need to be so just for a couple of hours to free himself from every female intrusion. He half closed the bathroom door and rested his hands on the washbasin, he stared into the mirror and scrutinising every line and wrinkle and greyish wisps of hair he tried to imagine in his mind the face of the old man. Five years, he thought, five years will come falling over me in future days like endless rain during a long winter, imagining Laura's face worried about the lines on his face, his wisps of greyish hair, his wrinkled skin and his hair turning whiter and whiter at the roots.

Looking at the tired, sleepy eyes of his image, Andrea suddenly became anxious and stood terrorised by the indelible and irreversible decadence that time had reserved for him.

VI

Laura's S-mail came the next morning just while Andrea was checking his on the computer. The message clearly stated he had to meet her at the railway station Porta Romana about midday but Andrea wanted to think twice before making a decision. Indeed this love for Laura had fallen on him so suddenly that Andrea wasn't so sure about how the girl felt about him. It could simply be love at first sight as it could also be a trick that Alberoni had put in place to build up his morale; the uncertainties started to multiply as the hot moments of the previous night came to mind. It had been fantastic without a doubt but the crisis Andrea was going through put him in a position of total scepticism since Laura worked for the Company and was part of that society that Andrea hated.

Anyway he didn't want to be impolite so he ended up waiting for her outside the station at the arranged time. It was a fresh Autumn Sunday; the sky was clear and weak rays of sunshine tried their best to warm the city. Andrea breathed in the fresh clean air and for an instant he felt happy and pleased. The station was busy with travellers coming and going. As it was Sunday there weren't any *pharmafarmers* or *ecoscouts* around, only people who yearned to get away from it all. Andrea on the other hand had no desire to go anywhere. He sat on the empty bench watching the hundreds of people who were coming down the main staircase to catapult to the nearest *transport*. Behind the long line of buses on the opposite side of the road, the main and most popular avenue in Milan opened up: Corso Porta Romana. It stretched as far as Piazza Duomo and traced a line between the two giants Amazon-Virgin and New Microsoft-Sony. That Sunday was a shopping day and the people roamed around, up and down carefree, stopping every now and then to contemplate the opulence of every shop window. Advertising banners and *dvd-screens* popped up like jack-in-a-box at every corner; colours and offers hit the eye, the right dose of psychological drug for joyous, naïve minds. There were also two rows of trees which disappeared into the horizon; two rows each side of such an intense green that dazzled the chromatic scale of the avenue. Down the middle there was the crowd wrapped up in their coats decorated with their material ornaments, an indefinite mass which ran the whole length of the avenue every day without ever going anywhere if not back to the starting point.

Andrea glanced here and there, then something about a hundred metres away caught his attention; on the corner of a software kiosk stood a man wearing a hat who was spying on him from behind a portable Opsolector. Andrea saw him clearly because he was the only one in that thick crowd of people to be staring at the station and he wondered if he was staring at him or was he imagining it.

'What are you thinking?' Laura broke in. The young girl was now sitting next to him, her hair was the same, the same eyes, the same beauty. Andrea was struck by lighting and fell silent, suspended between his thoughts and sensorial pleasure.

'What are you thinking?' repeated Laura.

'Nothing.' answered Andrea trying to deviate the topic.

'Sure?'

'Of course. Tell me, why this Sunday encounter?'

'For two reasons. First, I have to insert some data manually into the electronic brain at the station. Second, I wanted to see you.'

Andrea smiled but lacked confidence, not knowing what to say or do. He wanted to say and do lots of things yet he couldn't find anything worthwhile or certain. Laura liked him too; she was the perfect child of the Company who loved a natural but problematic child. Hard to believe. Could there really be something between the two of them? Maybe she too refuted the ideals of Global Corp. and saw Andrea as an ally. Or maybe the opposite. Andrea thought of his situation for a moment, then he turned around to look for the man in the hat but he had already disappeared into the crowd.

The two of them went straight in through the swing door across the long hall to the lift which had a sign on it saying 'Private'. The station was over crowded now with people going back and forth to the ticket desks. Besides the humming of the crowd, they could hear the heavy hammering of keys and the frantic emission of tickets; it was all very much like the process at Incubator Number 24. Andrea looked around him surprised by the large number of men and women who were ready to leave for some destination.

'Is the station always so crowded?' asked Andrea as he entered the lift.

'Of course!' answered Laura. 'You know the Monorail SV is then only means which takes you to the airport of Malpensa. No-one dares venture out of town on foot.'

The girl took her E-Id card out of her pocket and after putting it into the control panel, she pressed one of the many white keys. The doors closed instantly excluding the loud buzz coming from the hall. During then ride up Andrea didn't say a word, only the loud speaker spoke, announcing the twelve twenty five p.m. train for Moscow. The world was so close at hand yet so far away, thought Andrea. His curiosity to see the stretch of land between Milan and Malpensa was much stronger than travelling to Moscow where four identical *iperco-ops* and a Cedir covered in snow were waiting for him. The lift opened to the floor as quickly as it had closed and Andrea was brought back to reality, leaving his fantasy world of images and doubts behind him. He followed Laura down the silent and empty corridors and after a couple of turns they stopped in front of a blue panel and Laura finally said something.

'Here we are at the central switchboard.' exclaimed the girl.

She turned a lever and the panel opened up automatically revealing a complicated emerald green circuit. Taking a sort of small calculator from her pocket, she plugged it into the socket with a cable and started transmitting data. The passage of weightless bits was so swift that they scattered in the ethereal flow of electrons without impressing anything solid in the mind. Andrea felt the need to block that process, to break it down and finally see the missing passages which made everything so complex and superficial. Meanwhile, behind the corridor walls the machines continued working following the commands of the operators sitting comfortably in their offices. At the end of the corridor there was a small window and Andrea silently went up closer waiting for Laura to complete the operation. He looked outside and from there he could see platform 1 where the Monorail SV for Moscow was waiting for its passengers. The means of transport seemed alive, willing and ready to cover any distance; man had finally found his scapegoat for his sufferings at work. The electric engine whirred full of energy, it wasn't a sharp whir but rather slow and heavy. The noise sounded like the croaky voice of the old man and suggested a sense of age and use. Andrea realised that time passed even for machines and this destructive flow undermined their splendour and reliability.

'How does the Monorail SV engine manage to follow the schedule programmed by the computer so perfectly?' asked Andrea with a keen interest.

'I don't know that.' answered Laura putting the panel back in place. 'I came here only to update the system, not to make it work. It isn't my duty to know how the machines work. That's the duty of the engine drivers.'

Her answer was really disappointing, yet another proof of unmistakable automatism, but Andrea didn't let himself be influenced and wanted to get rid of any hesitation, to be confident, to be able to love this beautiful Milanese girl.

'Did you have a good time last night?' asked Andrea bearing a malicious smile.

Laura turned toward him and smiled. Then she moved closer to his ear.

'It was great!' she whispered and pushed him toward the lift.

Andrea was a bit upset and Laura saw it so she went closer and put her arms around his neck.

'Believe me, it was wonderful' continued the girl in a whisper. 'But this isn't the right time nor place to talk about it.'

On saying that she kissed him, took him by the hand and dragged him away out of the station.

Ten minutes later the young couple were surrounded by the fluctuating crowd in Corso Porto Romana. Hand in hand they both skipped left and right looking at the shop windows to see if there was anything interesting, Andrea found it hard to enjoy this rocking. There didn't seem to be time to stand still and reflect, only instinct had priority but even that didn't seem to have any real sense. Andrea breathed a sigh. He was still disappointed for not having found answers to his uncertainties. The place they were before, inside the station, was perfect to be alone together to talk; why on earth do men and women have to confess their sentiments in a bedroom? Andrea breathed another sigh. The sky was clear, it was a fresh Autumn Sunday, why destroy everything with this kibosh? The day was long and there would have been time to talk.

When they got to Piazza Duomo the matter had already been forgotten. An air balloon with its large tele-screen was flying up high over the city launching jingles similar to sweet melodies made to addict the people to their material cravings. Laura carried on window shopping without stopping and Andrea by her side read the announcements on the *dvd-screen*. The texts and images didn't completely match up, just like in real life when you try to grasp a shadow and lose the substance. Then there was a sudden hullabaloo and everybody in Piazza Duomo turned toward the mega *dvd-screen* where from a cloud of pixels the assuring face of the President of Global Corp. appeared.

'People of the World, best wishes for a Good Sunday to all of you!'

And on saying that he disappeared and the flow of TV adverts, music and news started up again.

'Long Live Global Corp.!' shouted Laura who stopped looking at the shop windows for a moment. Andrea watched her and followed her shouting out loud the famous motto. The girl smiled and moved up close to give him a second kiss. Andrea was flattered but also saddened because the way he was behaving wasn't his true individual inclination. It was really the crowd that told you what to do; the crowd was unbearable; praising the mega *dvd-screen* all together was unbearable too, and useless because the President of Global Corp didn't talk to you personally but to a mass void of expression, absent people from which the words bounced off like rubber marbles. Suddenly all the *dvd-screens* began to shout their mottos. Whoever stops is lost!; three for the price of two, throw away, don't bother repairing; a psychological influence that was really brainwashing for all the Milanese. How stupid, thought Andrea, but they won't make me stupid! I won't get caught out! He looked around and what he saw was a happy society, happy to be able to buy their stereos, happy to buy tons of tinned meat, happy to play tennis whenever they felt like it. Andrea however was sad because he had discovered the truth and it really was unbearable.

'Look at the love birds!' exclaimed several voices from behind Andrea and Laura.

The two turned round and found a happy group standing in front of them: Alberoni, accompanied by a blonde haired girl, and Manzetti who however didn't have any girlfriend with him.

'Where were you last night, eh?' asked Alberoni winking.

Andrea was about to answer when he suddenly felt Laura's pinch.

'We went for a walk, dear Alberoni' answered Laura.

Andrea was surprised. The two of them knew each other so his intuition wasn't altogether wrong. But why that pinch? It would have been nice to know what Laura was thinking inside her head, to manage to envisage the whole scene of what had happened in such a short time. The party, the lovemaking, the sleepless night, the mirror, the station, the *iperco-ops*, the President of Global Corp., the crowd. And just then in the crowd, between Alberoni's shoulder and his girlfriend, Andrea saw the man with the hat who had been spying on him from behind the Opsolector. This time he was even closer, but he was wearing a pair of dark Ray Ban sun glasses that hindered his view. Then a boy passed in front of him wearing a bright orange jacket and the man disappeared again making Andrea think he had imagined what he had seen.

'Pleased to meet you. Miriam.' said Alberoni's girlfriend. 'Something the matter?'

Andrea realised he had fallen into his usual thinking mode. Maybe the girl felt uncomfortable so he tried to put things right to avoid suspicious looks from Alberoni, Laura and the rest of them.

'Hey! Listen!' exclaimed Andrea with enthusiasm worthy of Alberoni 'Seeing as we are in front of the Amazon-Virgin store, how about going to the virtual cinema?'

Craftily he pointed to the Amazon-Virgin building. The CRS was not far away, an obvious way out.

'You're telepathic, Andrea!' said Alberoni. 'That's just what I was about to suggest!'

Andrea smiled shamelessly as if to say 'oh! what a coincidence!' but he hadn't a clue what film was showing. Anyway, he felt temporarily master of the situation and in a certain way thanked fate that had given him a favourable occasion. But was it his wit that had helped him or an even more intense force? Certainly, it was something stronger than a simple goods lift, stronger than the SV Monorail, stronger than the space shuttles, stronger than anything in the world. It was that undeniable strength that enabled the sun to rise and shine every day, the same strength which enabled his heart to beat every single moment of his life.

That week the virtual cinema was showing a variety of films as per usual but there had been great interest for the film 'Cosmopolitan'. The stalls were already full. Everyone was perched on red seats wearing metallic bands around their heads, ready to get lost in a reality which didn't exist on earth nor in heaven. The difference between virtual cinema and virtual relax was the fact that virtual relax was a personal choice made by the user while the cinema projected the spectator into a pre-programmed plot where there was a compulsory route to follow. The five sat in one of the front rows and waited for the film to start chatting among themselves while the black projection screen was getting ready. Andrea was sitting next to Laura.

'How come you know Alberoni?' asked Andrea in a low voice.

'I met him some time ago at a basketball tournament at the Public Gardens.' answered Laura keeping her eyes fixed on the screen. 'I haven't seen him since then. He's a friendly type but a bit too lively!'

Andrea grinned but felt perplexed. Laura really was a mysterious creature, difficult to get to know, with an insuperable barrier which made it difficult to tap into an absolute truth. She had secret desires, heated passions, weaknesses utterly unknown to him, and there was no point in trying to discover them, you could just take it or leave it. A bit like everything else. What was there behind the black projection screen? What was there behind the CEO's *dvd-screen*? It wasn't important, it didn't make any difference whatsoever; vague questions which were not worth answering. Andrea turned again to look at Laura out of the corner of his eye, just to see if there was any reaction, a sign that would reveal her feelings…nothing! In the meantime the metallic band had got into action, starting up everyone's images, filling up the absolute void.

The scene opens up in a devastated battlefield. A light mist hides masses of metal scattered over a large area of concrete. The smoke makes the air heavy and suffocating. The place seems abandoned but then from behind a van in flames springs out a man wearing a grey metallic suit. He is probably the Cosmopolitan, you can see it on his face: good looking, blond, with a perfect, well-toned body, and he seems to be covered with the Global Corp. seal everywhere. Then, after a close up of the Cosmopolitan, the scene rotates a hundred and eighty degrees to the opposite side where a group of well-armed men advances threateningly holding their coloured flag up high and chanting their song of war. The clash is inevitable. The group charges like a herd of barbarians yelling at the top of their voices and waving batons and sticks and knives; the Cosmopolitan however remains impassive with his feet firmly on the ground. The armed men charge him like mad men; one blow to the shoulder, a punch in the thigh but the Cosmopolitan resists returning punches and kicks; he answers back with vehemence at every blow and manages to protect all his vital parts and at the end they all fall one by one clenching their teeth for the pain and loss of strength. The scene ends with the Cosmopolitan standing on top of the burnt out van staring into the horizon with his lips near to a walkie talkie.

'The Patriots are all stone dead, it's another victory for the Cosmopolitan.'

His voice solemnly pronounces these words: it is a decisive voice, brave and determined. Then the title comes up on the screen.

Andrea wasn't very interested in following the story of the Cosmopolitan. He slept through most of it or rather he fell into a sort of half sleep when your mind perceives unconsciously. He saw the photograms of the film pass before him swiftly and he saw how they mixed with images and memories creating a sort of new plot and he thought again of the words of the old man and the flags the patriots had been waving with honour. Those flags represented nations, those states that had ethnic origin, language and traditions in common, but was this image of ruthless people, Global Corp wanted to give us, true? In past centuries had patriots really been barbarians armed to the teeth and thirsty for blood? Andrea wasn't completely convinced. He had already assisted to the manipulation of the past twice before; first with a song by the weather service, then with Alberoni's motto and now with this cinema scene which deep down enclosed a dangerous lie but which no-one seemed to worry about. Indeed the others weren't so easily distracted from the hypnotic flow of virtual reality; except for Andrea; they all preferred by far to follow the stunning adventures of the Cosmopolitan.

'Did you see that phenomenal jump he made from the patriot's helicopter? Spectacular!' Alberoni's voice echoed clearly around Galleria Vittorio Emanuele. Ever since they had left the Amazon-Virgin all he had done was talk about the film, how fascinating it was and Andrea nodded all the time trying desperately to talk to some of the others. He couldn't stand it any longer, not only because they talked too much but also because of the silly things he said, completely ignorant of the world around him. And Andrea kept silent, silent because it was too risky to make a comment on something which anyway wouldn't have changed a thing in the world. For now it was important to find the right personal balance, and passing in front of a Burger King, Andrea heard his tummy rumble like a hyper galactic rocket and his craving for food became an urgent need. Naturally, the croissant he had had in the morning together with all the reflections and thoughts could never satisfy him for a whole day!

'I'm feeling a bit peckish!' exclaimed Andrea rubbing his tummy as to imply a certain substantial hunger.

'Wait a bit, Andrea.' answered Manzetti calling him by name for the first time. 'Tonight we are having dinner at the Blue Moon!'

The Blue Moon. Not a bad idea after days on end of fast meals. It was time to enjoy the offer of a delicious meal. The five of them proceeded along the Galleria Vittorio and stopped at Piazza della Scala between the *transports* and the passers-by. The large roundabout was situated at the bottom of the fifteen floors of the McDonald-Nestlé and the Laurent-Chanel buildings.

From here a tunnel linked the *transport* stop with the other roads of Milan and there were no roads that separated the block of shops like Porta Romana, only corridors and lifts. Above the roundabout, however, a cylindrical area opened up; it stretched as far as the top of the *iperco-ops* and there, from out of a small dark blue circle, peeped some silver stars. The five Milanese chose one of the six lifts on the ground floor and started their ascent to the Blue Moon.

The entrance to the Blue Moon was an opaque glass door preceded by a spacious hall decorated with artistic elements of the Rising Sun and Art Nouveau. The floor was covered in a thick, soft blue and grey striped carpet whilst on the four walls, surrounded by cloisonné colours, there were moons with silent, melancholic faces, nothing at all like its real companion in the mysterious starry sky. Inside it had different characteristics. As soon as you entered there was a canary yellow room furnished with red armchairs and two or three Persian carpets. On the right there was the bar made completely out of wood and brass with landscape pictures and still life paintings; on the left there was the Blue Moon restaurant, designed in pure minimalist style with just the odd geometric decoration dotted here and there. Intense and soft lights contrasted in the right dose, creating an atmosphere in all three rooms. Manzetti was the first to separate from the group as he headed toward the waiter at the entrance to the restaurant. Alberoni and Miriam had gone to look at the large window and admire the wonderful view of Milan by night, while Laura made herself comfortable in an armchair adjusting her tight snake patterned trousers. Andrea couldn't help but watch her from a certain distance and feel the same thrill as the previous night. This girl manages to be elegant all the time, thought Andrea, and he went toward her with a phlegmatic step waiting for her to notice him.

'Aren't you going to sit down?' asked Laura without looking up.

'It doesn't matter.' answered Andrea. 'It'll soon be our turn.'

He pointed to Manzetti, and just as he turned to look at him, he saw Marco enter through the main door. It seemed as if a long time had passed, even an eternity, since the last time he had seen his friend, and a lot had happened since then but an evening wouldn't be enough to list all of it.

'It's our turn!' he exclaimed at a certain point to Laura. The girl had lifted her head up and Andrea's eyes crossed her splendid eyes and he smiled.

'Go on ahead.' he said with a sensual voice full of emotion. 'I've got to say hello to a certain person.'

He was about to leave her when she grabbed him by his arm. It was the same grip as the pinch, a strong grasp, impulsive and at the same time binding like a chain which prevents you from flying up over the ceiling and beyond.

'Aren't you going to give me a kiss?' asked Laura with her sweet eyes.

Andrea felt slightly embarrassed but he couldn't resist those blue eyes and those lips so overflowing with passion and so he popped a kiss on her mouth. A quick kiss, short-lived but with the same intensity as the other night, as if it were his very first pang of love full of vigour and naturalness. Andrea looked into her eyes again then he turned quickly and headed for the bar next door.

Marco was at the bar, absorbed in his reading on the Opsolector. Andrea walked up to him slowly and took him by surprise just like Marco had done to him four days earlier.

'It'd be nice to visit the ISS!'

Marco turned around scared and Andrea worried to see his tired face. A pale white on which his eyes looked like bottomless pits.

'Ah, it's you! Hi!' replied Marco resuming his reading on the Opsolector.

Andrea realised there was something wrong and noticed that Marco wasn't really concentrating on the words and images that came up on the screen of the Opsolector.

'What are you reading?' asked Andrea aiming at starting a conversation without appearing too nosey.

'Nothing.' answered Marco with no change in his tone of voice, disheartened and bored. 'News, surveys, advice, scandals, the usual. Besides, today I went to see my parents.'

The sentence, said with a certain emphasis and put at the end of the answer, seemed as if he wanted to communicate something and Andrea remembered immediately the same sentence he said during their last meeting. Maybe his parents were the cause of his problems? Andrea wasn't sure and intended to get to the bottom of the problem not because Marco was an old friend in search of consolation but because this situation could be another useful clue, another step in the right direction toward an unknown goal into which he put all his trust.

'Do you remember fifteen years ago?' began Andrea hoping to boost up the morale of both. 'When I met your father for the first time and I was an absolute idiot? Well they were great times…'

'I don't want to go down memory lane!' interrupted Marco. 'Tell me instead what you've done today and what you're planning for tomorrow!'

'Nothing. I haven't done anything special and I won't be doing anything tomorrow. Why don't you want to talk about past times and about what you haven't done?'

Andrea felt proud for such a touching sentence coming out of his mouth. A booming and irrevocable sentence just like those spoken by the old man.

'That's what my parents always say!' muttered Marco with a deep bitterness. 'They say I haven't followed certain things which they call "ideals". Is it my fault if I can't get rid of how I am a slave of the things around me? I realise it, dear Andrea. We are slave to things.'

The words reached Andrea's ears heavily and seriously, and he was bewildered.

'What do you mean?' he said in a hesitant voice.

As much courage as he might have had, it was difficult to look harsh truth in the face, and face the abyss of such deep thoughts. Andrea was taken by surprise by the boomerang effect of his words and for the first time he had confirmation that in all these years Marco too, had harboured resentment toward Global Corp., or rather, toward such a shallow world that called itself Global Corp.

'In such a short time everything we buy has started to control us as if unforgiving tyrants and we don't throw anything away for any reason in the world.'

Marco was on the verge of banging the Opsolector on the bar but he didn't and Andrea was struck by the seriousness on Marco's tired face. He saw an aspect of him he had never seen before in all his life and in a flash the old joys of the past became over shadowed, showing how truth could be changeable and complex. The old images of Marco smiling, immortalised in who knows which ideal, happy figure, took on for Andrea, the characteristics of something alien or unrelated.

'I have always been tied to the external world neglecting what I feel inside. We all wish to travel in life and simultaneously we plunge more and more into domestic traps. We accumulate just enough to weigh ourselves down and keep us tied to one place. And we can't accuse anyone but ourselves because although the theme of escape is ideal, we prefer to limit our choices to give us a sense of security. At this point I wonder: how much time has they stolen from us?'

Collapse is inevitable. Noisy, devastating like an avalanche of debris and bricks. What a load. So many purchases. Andrea had admired everything. He had admired how his life had been a series of accumulation in search for objects to fill space and time, and now all that nice furniture in the old man's hiding place was losing value and disintegrating into a cloud of dust under the unsustainable weight of incoherence. Andrea painfully realised how he had wasted time with the old man but he didn't want to accept the new reality for fear that this was another lie leaning on hundreds of other small, white lies.

'You're wrong.' responded suddenly Andrea grasping at yet another pretext. 'Nobody can steal your inner wealth.'

Marco didn't say a word leaving Andrea dejected. There was so much delusion now that Marco listened to his boastful statements in silence with a melancholic disapproval. That severe and final silence was too hard to swallow and it was useless to look in other directions once cornered. On the one hand the robotic barman continued to shake drinks and clean glasses with such coldness just like the tin he had been made from and on the other hand the customers at the bar just sat and chatted in peace. Driven by the urgent need to escape, Andrea wandered with his eyes until he saw a well-known figure get up from his table near the bar entrance. He had just taken off his cap and a pair of dark glasses but Andrea recognised him immediately and was surprised to see a pink shaved head appear from under the cap. The spy-man was none other than one of those vandals who had attacked him a fortnight ago, The Men of the Night. The damn Men of the Night. What did they say that night? He still remembered it. What are you doing around at this time of night? Well don't you know it can be dangerous?

Andrea was fuming, he felt like clenching his fist against the wall just to let off steam. But he had to remain calm because not all was lost. To know the identity of the man with the hat could be the long awaited clue, another step allowing him to complete the unstable step that Marco had taken. It was important to keep calm and move quickly.

'Listen Marco.' said Andrea quickly. 'I have to leave for a moment. Don't disappear like last time, please.'

Marco nodded distractedly but Andrea didn't wait for an answer and moved straightaway to follow the young skin head. Marco kept silent and sat still by the bar with a worried look staring into space. And if this inner wealth, these damn ideals, aren't as important as they are made out to be? Wouldn't it be better to cancel them in order to be happy? He took two deep sighs, resigned. He then took his hat and put it on so that he could hide the expression on his face from the others. He left silently, with the Opsolector under his arm and his Ray Ban in his pocket. He disappeared again into the inexplicable world of the misunderstood.

In the meantime Andrea, having just left the Blue Moon, catapulted into the labyrinth of corridors of the McDonald-Nestlé. The young skin head moved quickly but without his hat he was easy to identify in the crowd. Andrea began to stalk him keeping at a certain distance for safety; the chase lasted quite a while but Andrea never lost sight of the man. Going through corridors, down escalators and across landings, the two came to the western end of the McDonald-Nestlé. At that moment neither of them perceived the whirring noise of the cameras that were following their every movement from every angle, zooming in and recording them minute after minute. The chase continued outside where the roads were still in pre Darkening and even here far from the lights of the *iperco-ops*, the video cameras continued filming nonstop from their orbital position miles away. Indeed the GPS satellites moved threateningly, endlessly checking every single movement on the earth's surface. The real spies were the invisible ones, the ones that listened and observed everything without anyone ever being able to prove that there really was someone behind that scrutinising, undaunted lens. Even if the elaboration of a simple thought was by far the hardest work for the heavy electronic structure, it was impossible to escape the vigilant stare of Global Corp.

The young skinhead still wasn't aware of Andrea and continued obliviously toward who knows which destination. Andrea had never lost sight of him and had put all his effort into keeping up with him to find out the absolute truth and satisfy his curiosity, to find the hiding place of the Men of the Night. However, he was also thirsty for revenge which was gnawing at him and made him come out of hiding much earlier than he should have. As soon as they were in a badly lit area on the road, Andrea sprung out of nowhere and jumped onto the young skin head hitting him violently on the back of his neck. The victim moaned and fell to the ground. Andrea didn't give him a chance to breathe and he pulled him up to get a good look at his face.

'Oh! Look who's here then! Where are your friends now, eh?'

The young vandal opened his eyes and even if he was still stunned, he clearly saw the angry face of Andrea.

'Who the devil are you?' shouted the young man scared. 'What do you want from me? Leave me alone!'

His acute voice almost made Andrea laugh but he had to be careful not to be seen by indiscreet eyes and he immediately stopped him from yelling.

'Stop pretending! Confess! Is that how you get your kicks? Spying and mugging folk?'

'What on earth are you talking about? I don't know anything about it!'

The young skin head denied every charge hoping he was convincing.

'Don't talk shit!' shouted back Andrea. 'Where is the Opsolector and the Ray Ban, bastard?'

He tugged at him a couple of times and looked him straight in the eye raging.

'I haven't got anything! I don't have a thing!'

The young skin head was dead scared and shook like a leaf as he stood there held in Andrea's clutches. He didn't look at all like a tough guy but more like a young kid unable to defend himself. He didn't show any resistance nor did he try to run off; on the other hand he treated Andrea as the delinquent. Precisely for this reason Andrea was taken by surprise once more by the boomerang effect of his actions, and surprised by the skin head's reaction, he loosened his grip. The young skin head wriggled himself free and fell to the ground again but he got up quickly and ran off without saying a word or even turning to look back. On reaching the end of the road the skin head began to shout for help.

'Help, police! Help! A Man of the Night!'

Andrea soon realised what was happening so he took shelter in the darkness accompanied by the sirens of the Darkening. Doubt is the truth. The Men of the Night don't exist.

VII

'The Men of the Night don't exist' confirmed the old man perched on his chair at the desk. 'It's a simple urban legend! Global Corp. invents all kinds of things.'

His voice echoed slightly around the thick walls of his room, which was lit by feeble candle- light, still living as always in semi darkness. Shadows threw themselves like trembling ink blots behind objects and ledges, taking on the strangest of shapes. The furniture was still in the same place, with the same awfulness, the same austerity of dark, dull wood. Remembering the contradiction made evident by Marco, Andrea saw how everything had changed quickly and were still changing. The meeting with the old man, the revelations on the external world, the involvement in Milanese life, the new aspects of the external world and finally the dissolution of the exterior world; truth had changed its face several times not because someone had changed the rules of the game but because the human mind was not such a greatly reliable thing to base one's existence on.

'There's one thing I don't understand.' resumed Andrea after a short reflection. 'All this story is fruit of the imagination then, isn't it?'

'It is, in a certain way.' answered the old man.

'Well then, all those discussions we had about creativity and mental work, what good has it done? Global Corp. uses the same arms that man should use to fight it. At this point I don't think it makes sense to consider it an enemy.'

'Interesting question! I see you have thought about it over the last few days so let me answer you as best I can.'

The old man got up from his chair barely holding onto its wobbly arm; it looked as if he had lost all his strength in just a few days and he could hardly move. Andrea followed his movements slowly and he saw him open a large cupboard full of heavy volumes of knowledge. The wood squeaked once again as the old man pulled out a dusty copy by Dante Alighieri, but this time Andrea didn't have the same curiosity as before and languished at the thought of having to repeat the same lecture. Enough reflection, his brain was totally fused.

'A long time ago' continued the old man 'there was a kind of organization called Church.'

Andrea tended his ear. The old man hadn't even opened the book yet and he had already started explaining; Andrea enjoyed listening to his memories of a far off epoch, he liked to listen to these stories beyond all conformity so he sat listening and waiting for the joy of a new emotional discovery.

'Visual communication, with its emotional suggestions of sacred art, was a fundamental vehicle that the worshipper had to look t to understand the meaning according to the oral teachings of the Church. But it was a teaching given by the Church itself, not imagined by the faithful worshippers. In the same way Global Corp. imparts its teachings to the sweet embryos of the pre-Alpha group.'

'Did the Church project coloured images onto screens and invent urban legends?' asked Andrea in an almost childish tone.

'Not really!' answered the old man. 'The Church used stained glass windows and believed in an almighty and omniscient power that said had created the whole world. He was called God.'

The scene suggested many ideas; the wise man who laughed at the funny questions that the inexpert disciple continually proposed.

'Where is this God?' continued Andrea playing the part of the inexpert disciple.

'Everywhere.' answered the old man making a wide and majestic gesture with his arm. 'He is the invisible, immanent power. In fact we don't notice His presence very much. Dante himself tried to see Him, to hear Him. Read this!'

The old man opened the book at the halfway mark and pointed at a series of verses with his wrinkly finger. Andrea moved closer to read.

O thou, Imagination, that dost steal us
So from without sometimes, that man perceives not,
Although around may sound a thousand trumpets,

Who moveth thee, if sense impel thee not?
Moves thee a light, which in the heaven takes form,
By self, or by a will that downward guides it.

I don't understand a word!, thought Andrea. The jumbled up words didn't communicate anything to him but for the odd word. 'Imagination', 'a thousand trumpets', 'moveth thee a light', the rest was lost in the flow of these archaic phrases. And the old man continued to talk and talk and talk and rattle on.

'When he says "moveth thee a light", he is describing a sort of luminous fount which lives in the sky and transmits ideal images...'

'Yes, but what is it for anyway?' Andrea brusquely interrupted. 'What man imagines isn't real so it doesn't produce anything. Ideals are useless and illusory. If anything memories can be useful because they are images coming from real experiences.'

Andrea hid behind his claims following a route of his own. For a long time now he had withdrawn into himself and gradually his relationships with the external world had changed. Intimacy with just one person could cause this – it emptied the world of friends, provoked disgust for dialogues with other people, making everyday life somewhat unreal and rather equivocal.

'It's true,' answered the old man. 'And it is for this reason I have not followed God.'

Andrea was puzzled yet again and felt a great delusion in seeing the personality of the old man change from being a stable pillar to a moveable block and continually changing. Just like all the others, the old man too had disoriented him with unexpected surprise, creating increased doubt and also he hadn't stopped contradicting himself with his antinomies, shuffling the young Milanese's opinions. Indeed if God were an ideal, why did the old man deny God and at the same time promote the ideal? It did not make sense, it hardly held up on such shaky and insecure pillars. So with what right did this man think he could criticise everything and take the place of Global Corp. which was so confident, determined and never subject to change? The strange thing was the placidity with which he old man presented himself. Over confident. Too sure of himself. Surely, this man, to reach this balance, must have had to fight the same battle Andrea was fighting, perhaps against God instead of against Global Corp., but no sign could transpire to suggest the intense suffering of a troubled life. What had he been through really in his life? Was it all fiction or reality? The actors raise the curtain, it is true, they play the scene, they jump and giggle, but that tragic moment always comes when it is necessary to pull down the mask covering their faces.

'Now that I think about it,' continued the old man. 'There is something written by a certain Leopardi about recollections…'

That was the moment when Andrea exploded. He could no longer hold back in front of the old man's literary ramblings, he needed to see, hear and, why not, reach out and touch it

'Your discourses are just words that fly!' muttered Andrea suddenly. 'You've got old furniture, old pieces of paper, thick old books, but what have you done in your life? What ideals did you follow and put into practice? What is there beyond this abstract explanation?'

On saying this he moved his hands pointing to the shelves packed with knowledge. He realised he had moved onto a topic different to the one he had started with but he was still mad after his discussion with Marco.

'There must be something!' exclaimed Andrea. 'Why don't you tell me about your life, old man?'

The old man wasn't offended by this derogatory term but seemed aware that sooner or later the conversation would have got to this critical stage. Andrea was surprised by how the old man's calmness didn't let the storm devastate his seas.

'You're right!' answered the old man without breaking down in a soft voice. 'Pragmatism, not idealism. If you want to hear the eye witness testimony of the past, if this is what you really want, well, sit down and listen to me.'

The old man took the usual two glasses and poured out the wine. Then, having all Andrea's attention on him when spirits had calmed down, he began to tell his story.

'I don't believe it is important where and when I was born.' started up the old man. 'However, I think it is right to tell you I'm from this area. My father was a farm worker in the Padan Plain, a hardworking man who had worked hard all his life for our family. He said he was part of the workforce and he often taught me things about his job. One day, while I was walking in the countryside, he told me about workers and explained the socialist ideology to me in detail which in his times was very fashionable all over Europe. I was just twelve I remember and I didn't take much interest in politics but I was fascinated by things he told me. This ideology spoke of an equal society without either rich or poor, without injustices or discrimination and prophesied a serene and peaceful world…'

Andrea stopped to think about his words for a while; the world of Global Corp. was serene and peaceful, it was a world without rich or poor. Why wasn't the old man satisfied of seeing his father's dream realised? Andrea preferred to put him a question at another time so he continued to listen to the story in silence.

'…At that time there was a heated debate on this topic between socialism and capitalism. My father said this contrast between the two factions was something secular and seemed never ending. According to him, socialism was more important because it impressed fundamental values into man like the love of work, the communion of wealth, well anyway, a sense of virtue and brotherhood. Capitalism, on the other hand, was seen as something oppressive even if it was a system widely used in all the Western countries. The fact remains that the second half of the twentieth century was a devastating mark for socialism. With the strengthening of capitalism and the rapid development of automatism, man began to get lazier, more spoilt, more of a victim of comfort offered by capitalist well-being. The way of life became an ever increasing "artificialisation" and when the digital age came along at the beginning of the century, man was reduced to pressing buttons on a keyboard without any real contact with the real world any more. Today none of the striking results of that digital process is the *transports*, remote controlled vehicles which don't require any physical or mental effort by man; or the *dvd-screens*, which became weavers of deception attributing the power of the people to people emptied, inept and degenerated. At the end lack of ideas reigns and while reality is getting more complicated and the complexities increase dramatically, minds become simplified and men lose all their rationality. This was the situation more or less, in the first ten years of the century and my father, outraged by such a "crisis of values", hoped for a turning point. I was growing up with certain ideas, thinking that what my father had told me was right and I continued my studies diligently without realizing that the world around me was changing. Socialism was disappearing and just a few unrelated groups remained to follow the concept of revolution against the conservative classes, no-one had the strength any longer to change the world. But the world was changing. It could be seen from the road, in the shops, in the houses; everything was collapsing without making the slightest noise. Without desiring it, history took me to reliving in first person a period of protest and revolt which involved the first thirty years of the twenty-first century. Fortunately, my father died before the worst happened. In 2009 I finally managed to get my degree in classic studies and I started teaching at the university straightaway. If I don't error it was the autumn of the same year when I met the Commies for the first time…'

The name didn't sound at all new to Andrea. Several years previously, Marco's father had spoken about them during one of the frequent Sunday meetings at the *gerial*. It often happened that he would tell stories to his two friends about the existence of the Commies so that the name of the group had taken on a mystic and legendary meaning for Andrea. The Commies were followers of an old movement that waved the red flag in favour of those who made machinery work, or at least that was what Marco's father used to say.

'…At the beginning it was just a game to me, a simple and innocent participation in political life which was supposed to please my father up in Heaven, but soon the situation worsened and I realised too late that I was in serious trouble. In the summer of 2022 after a series of protests spread over the previous years, the spark that would change the course of events finally went off. The revolt naturally exploded in France where for quite a while everyone had been rebelling against every decision taken by the centralised state. The French began to ask for a European collegial identity instead of the *exception française*; they were demanding a strong and dynamic economy capable of eliminating the traditional, protectionist and oppressive state completely. "Fewer taxes" and "decentralisation" were the key words that were being shouted in the red hot streets of Paris. Then from France through Europe, the reprisals multiplied simultaneously in every corner of the earth and so soon the message reached the ears of everyone. The blood of millions of people was shed in rivers, brought together by the same proposal, that of changing the world. So as not to betray my friends, I decided to take part in the rebellions too, to attack that old system once and for all and destroy it forever. But the fire of rebellion was destined to burn out eight years later when the largest international companies made their strategic move. In 2030 Global Corp. got the best of the situation and got a very different result from the one they were expecting. Strangely it wasn't a repressive counter-revolution. It was more than anything else a solution to the crisis which was deteriorating the international market and the lives of each and every individual. With the aim of improving the situation and make things more liveable, it was necessary to break off every relation with the past and therefore the State, symbol of ancient traditions, had to be eliminated and globalised. From that moment every old habit or custom, every organization or infrastructure from the past lost its true identity, merging with the new multicultural civilization. Really, no-one had asked for globalization but there just wasn't enough material time to prevent the process already underway. The end of the crisis and the institution of a new system satisfied the demands of the people and most accepted the new conditions promptly; others however weren't that convinced with the newly adopted method, they preferred to continue fighting, this time in honour of their country and anti-globalisation. France replied saying, "We are becoming a country like all the others", but the appeal passed unobserved seeing that each country was absorbed in the melting pot of a global confederation. Local and national governments disappeared rapidly and soon the *iperco-ops* and entrepreneurships signed Global Corp. sprang up. Thus the new world was born and during the Years of Change great reconstruction works were started up...'

The news was so surprising, not very precise, but surprising; an epoch of real chaos out of which Global Corp. passed itself off as the saviour. The question was spontaneous: was the solution adopted by Global Corp. the best one, even if it had given decades of prosperity later on? Andrea realised how but he didn't understand why.

'...In the end the Masbuild buildings touched the sky and technology finally defeated nature. Cities began to get bigger and bigger due to the Maxi-urbanisation and the era of mass genetic engineering started up. The remaining few who disagreed with Global Corp., the Commies in particular, hid in the countryside and they lost track of them in who knows what poky places. But I was too old to be getting dragged into other scuffles. I was too weary to carry on fighting; however I didn't intend to get swept away by Global Corp. so I took what few things I had managed to rustle up during the Years of Change and I hid away here in the old and forgotten ruins of St. Ambrogio church. I didn't have the chance to know what had happened to my friends, I thought that one day I would have left this place, but time has taken all my strength away and before I knew it I was unable to understand the new generation of humanity that now marches proud and carefree on the metropolitan streets. Having given up I stayed within these walls to think and think again. Counting the losses and assessing the damage…'

Pause. Or rather, a long and permanent interruption. The old man kept his head lowered in the darkness, absorbed by his thoughts. Tied to promises that had never been made and obedient to laws that had long gone and were no longer in use, the old man sat in silence on his rickety chair. It was a sad story, painful, but Andrea didn't fully appreciate the conclusion of the facts. There was something which didn't fit in, perhaps another hidden contradiction between the words and events; this obsession with trying to find the error was devouring him and totally obscured the true reasons of the heart.

'And the Church?' asked Andrea breaking the silence. 'What happened to the Church in all this turmoil?'

His question had a specific aim: shed light on the old man's mistakes. The only confirmation could be obtained by going back to his initial discourse, the one about God and the Church.

'The Church is a symbol of the past.' answered the old man calmly. 'And so it disappeared with everything else. It disappeared in silence in 2043 when it realised it had lost its role in the world. The aid of Global Corp. arranged things so that the world population put their trust in the President of Global Corp. and no longer in an abstract God hidden up in the skies. I don't like today's world at all, I realise it would have been better to preserve the world instead of changing it.'

'Well then I was right to say that ideals are useless and illusory. Listen to me, it's much better to keep your feet on the ground.'

Andrea's words began to take on a tone of voice with a certain confidence. He had never felt so sure of himself in all his life.

'Believing in an ideal isn't useless; following what you believe in means following the reason why you exist, it means to live!'

The old man always had an answer ready on the tip of his tongue and this prophesising highlighted even more the pleasure of the challenge that Andrea had secretly set up.

'I don't need God nor socialism to live. All I need is food and money in large amounts, only this way can we satisfy all our desires.'

'Live according to your own needs, eh?' said the old man in a pungent tone. 'Following your impulses, hot, immediate and emotionally thrilling; a way of life typical of a child who eats when he feels like it, wakes up and satisfies his needs as he feels fit without any reflection or responsibility. If you start off as a baby and carry on like this until you are grown up, working and enjoying yourself this way, well, your life will be nothing but shabby and distracted with has no thoughts to believe in. Believing means living your life to the full, it means giving a sense to everything you do. Remember there is always something to believe in. Whatever it is. It's up to you to choose and not regret the choices you have made. My father was wrong or perhaps I was wrong in interpreting him, anyway I have finally realised that the real solution is to stay tied to tradition, the family, the homeland, to those things that are the most certain things we have in this world, although their roots get lost in the mist of time.'

Andrea didn't bat an eyelid in front of the old man's peremptory judgments, he knew he had an advantage on his side. The old man could carry on preaching his fantasies, but seeing as he had contradicted himself, there was no chance he would still be believed. First, he said the world should change, then he said he preferred to stat tied to the old traditions; talking like this not only had he wasted his breath but also the strength that kept his noble spirit alive. Andrea has admired him in every situation but now, seeing his drama, he realised the old man was nothing but a man with his own mistakes and weaknesses; just like Andrea who had read and re-read the *ekletto-encyclopaedia* only to lose all confidence and give way to a world of anxiety. Concrete imperfection, man-made imperfection, which didn't have a place in the perfect world of Global Corp. Andrea then remembered the straight white teeth of the young nurse, the melodic laughter of Alberoni, Laura's seductive legs; he remembered the carefree race in the orphanage, the strolls in the Public Gardens, the virtual pleasures of CRS, and in commemorating such happiness, the happiness of a peaceful life, Andrea made a drastic decision.

'You have disappointed me!' shouted Andrea clenching his fist.

The old man didn't say anything.

'You have disappointed me!' repeated Andrea in a louder voice. 'I hope I never see you again!'

The old man didn't say anything and kept his gaze fixed in space. He didn't see Andrea jump up, he didn't see him furiously knock the glass onto the floor, he didn't hear the glass shatter against the wall, he didn't hear the shards of glass fall to the ground; some paper flew into the air but the old man didn't say a word and he let the young Milanese leave to go to where he came from. It was the end, nothing but the end. Some minutes passed, long minutes which seemed like eternity and when silence returned to the room the old man moved his eyes. They moved slowly through the dark until he set his eyes on the doorway. There, a few centimetres away from the darkness of the corridor a white candle lay covered in a blanket of dust; it lay there muffled, tired, broken in two, as proof that everything was bound to end, both life and dreams. The old man gave another glance then he suddenly felt very tired and felt a tremendous pain in his heart.

In those few minutes Andrea had gone far, further than expected. The siren of the Darkening with its lament had been ringing for some time now and the dark had swallowed up the empty, silent streets just like every night. Andrea had stopped every contact with the outside world and was busy mulling over what had just happened; he had been waiting for a while for his moment of glory and he had been easily pleased, but after showing his self-determination with the old man, he no longer felt that thrill, that satisfaction one gets when you have reached your goal. On the contrary bitterness and rancour troubled him. Certainly the old man had made a mistake and so a myth had fallen but maybe Andrea's behaviour was over the top, a bit too severe. The old man wasn't the real enemy to fight, confronting his ideas had been quite useless seeing as how the situation had worsened now. Andrea felt heavy at heart and regretted having acted in the wrong way. Too late to remediate, too late to turn back; he was already walking quickly and was now way beyond the Duomo without realizing it. There was nothing left to do but go back home with regret and bear the inner pain that would become much worse and unbearable.

When he got to his apartment in the middle of the night, Andrea was exhausted and a heavy harrowing began to pulse in his head. Andrea felt as if his heart had suddenly ended up in his brain, he felt the thumping at his temples and every beat went from one side of his head to the other. Stabiliser, he needed a dose of stabiliser, it was the only cure for such pain. Unfortunately there wasn't even a single dose of the precious liquid in his room. He opened up cupboards, drawers. No stabilizer in sight. Andrea shrugged his shoulders and decided to forget the matter as he sat on the bed. Doing his best to bear the pain he closed his eyes and pressed his hand on his forehead with all his strength to get rid of the continuous hammering. His head was on the verge of exploding but he couldn't do anything about it. He bent his head down in the grip of another pain then he lifted it up and saw the last thing he would have ever expected to see: the red diary. It had been left open on his desk since Friday and since then he hadn't even thought of looking through it. It had been only two days but in those two days lots had happened and even more during the whole week. Remembering, Andrea came up with other flashbacks. What had the old man said to him? You need to feel hurt and upset inside otherwise you can't formulate the right sentences that will penetrate like x-rays. Modern medicine often took great advantage of x-rays to cure patients. Would writing great words in that diary have the same effect? In case of emergency you are not allowed to think twice. Andrea wasn't thinking at all but he instinctively took his pen in hand and started writing in the hope that his nightmare, his torment, would end as quickly as possible.

And so it was. He suddenly fell asleep over half a page of writing. He fell asleep serenely dreaming the night sky and tree-lined valleys never seen before. All fruit of his imagination which galloped through the sky, beyond the invisible walls of Milan, in those poky places where the Commies were sheltering, abandoned by man and now covered in moss and rust. The wooden shelter was in some part of the valley, surrounded by dark green. It was the same place where Andrea had previously been busy making that mysterious object. This time however there was no clay mass nor any sketchy form. In their place was a beautiful vase which shone in the darkness of the shelter. It was beautiful. The potter's wheel continued to turn and Andrea stared at the object shocked by its singular beauty. He was pleased with himself at having managed to finish something so great, an object of his own creation, even if simple. It was much better than all the prefabricated models. The carving was perfect, the patterns moved like gentle synchronised waves interspersed with floral images, but this wasn't a standard product of a machine, this was the result of human spirit and his capacity to model and transform something insignificant into an object of splendid beauty. Andrea wouldn't have been ashamed to show this vase to the world because by revealing his unique personality he would have freed himself at last. Free.

On this note, the sky thundered threateningly behind him scaring him to death. The unexpected shock made him lose control of the moment and the potter's wheel started to turn even faster. The effects of his mistake were immediate and devastating. The vase began to turn on itself going crazy and in a flash it wilted before Andrea's eyes. Handfuls of clay broke off and flew everywhere, One bit ended up on the walls while another bit hit Andrea in the eye and the pain was awful. The young Milanese soon felt the hot flames flare up in his eye sockets and slowly he felt the fire burning, burning, getting hotter and hotter.

Andrea woke up panting with his heart beating. Drops of sweat trickled down his forehead and his whole body was in a cold sweat after that sudden reawakening. Silence. Everything was turned off, everything was quiet. His headache had gone together with his dream and now his head was completely empty, like a sharp, silent weapon. Nothingness tore at Andrea's heart inflicting the worst pain, the worst guilt. The point of no return had been overcome.

VIII

Andrea had never felt so sad and alone. Everyone seemed so indifferent to his state of inner suffering, and waking up to a Monday morning rain contributed to making his day even more grey than it was. Andrea could hardly open his eyes scared by the idea of having to face the emptiness of another week. The dark was awaiting him, darkness again with its invisible cloak making every surface opaque. Strangely the lighting hadn't turned on. The crystal liquid clock struck eight thirty but the lighting hadn't come on. The only light came from the window, from the light of the grey covered clouds. Andrea didn't move, he just lay there waiting for his pupils to get used to the poor light. His face was resting on the empty white pages of the diary. He felt their slight roughness against his cheek, he could smell their staleness, and then he saw some letters written in a disorderly fashion on half a page. The writing looked hurried and jumbled up and Andrea was sure it was another message coming from his obscure subconscious.

Letter IV – Milan 13th November 2073

<u>*Sonnet to Existence*</u>

And places still to be seen
Will change human life,
Because man is weak, lost
Dissolved in the fluctuating crowd;
Isn't this perhaps the end of a snowflake,
Fallen on the indistinct mantle candid and soft?
I do not mean to break nature's course
I do not mean to despise such vision of the world,
But I beg destiny,

Andrea lifted his head swiftly and rubbed his eyes. What big words! What wonderful words! The old man's formula had produced its effects and here on these inert pages commanded words whose sense suggested the incredible. Reading those sentences, Andrea was, to say the least, amazed. Such a composition couldn't certainly be his and yet it was he who had written it. Although he had gone against the old man, at the end, he had taken the same road as him, that alternative road anti-Global Corp., that individual road that is indicated to you but you take it alone. Enough being the simple member of a hated society! Andrea wanted to be something better, something different. And those lines in the diary were the proof. Caught by last night's torture, Andrea had finally managed to create something original, to put words together whose meaning went beyond all his expectancies.

However a bit of confusion still remained in his sleepy head. His non-stop thinking had been like an electric shock that had fused his brain, and soon after nothing was left except for regretting having had an argument with the old man. Unfortunately there was no turning back. His headache had been the breaking point with everything and like an atomic bomb it had only brought emptiness. Up until now he had made his bizarre choices and had got some surprising results but now that the grace had been given, what lay between him and the future? Andrea had the vague certainty that things wouldn't be the same as before. The fact that he hadn't gone into work threw a dark shadow onto his trustworthy condition. Why hadn't the lights come on? It was the first time the lighting hadn't worked, or better still it had never happened in all the life history of Global Corp. that the electric system failed to carry out its synchronised programme. Perfection shot in the heart. Andrea sniggered at the thought and got up to check the main board. To his dismay! Next to the door to his room (where the mains were usually installed) the door had been almost ripped off and instead of the control panel, there was a mass of jumbled wires and broken circuits as if someone had knocked into the mains board with their shoulders. Andrea took a step forward but a sudden spark convinced him to stay where he was and wonder who had done such a thing. Not having any electricity, Andrea took his mobile and linked up to his computer to check the satellite security system. No evidence of a break-in, no presence had been registered lately except for Andrea. This could only mean one thing, that Andrea was the only person to enter the room in the last twelve hours and was the only person to blame for that action. Was it really him who had broken the mains? Andrea felt a certain perplexity and tried to remember step by step what had happened the previous night. He fell asleep, he dreamt, he woke up again in the middle of the night. And then? A bank of fog stretched from the first to the second awakening, an unbridgeable emptiness that had sucked up all Andrea's sense of security. Was it really him who broke the electricity mains? If this was the truth, well then, there was a lot to worry about because it really was a crazy thing to do. Deprive oneself of a convenient necessity, how stupid! Then Andrea remembered Marco's words, and when his mobile rang, he was startled. It was Laura; only then did Andrea remember he had dumped his friends the night before, and that was another burden, another permanent, unforgettable scar on the skin of his weak spirit.

'He...Hello?' said Andrea in a weak, hesitating voice.

'Hello?! Andrea? It's Laura.'

Her voice sounded different over the phone.

'What on earth happened to you last night? I looked for you everywhere. You disappeared like a ghost.'

Andrea didn't quite know what to say. He certainly couldn't say he had had an experience with a crazy old man and then he composed a poem in the grip of a terrible head ache. It didn't make sense to him. Imagine Laura's reaction! No, it wasn't the case to tell her the truth, but his life wasn't so exciting to involve him in many activities, and it was difficult to find a plausible excuse. He said the first thing that came to mind. A fresh and harmless lie to cover his true actions.

'I met a friend and he invited me to play Laser Tennis. You know, I hadn't seen him for ages so I decided to accept. I wanted to tell you but then there wasn't time…'

'Your voice sounds strange, Andrea? Do you feel ok?'

'Yeah, yeah…' answered Andrea quickly.

He needed to make it a quick conversation.

'What about you? What did you do?'

The flash question had a precise aim. Hurry up the conversation or change topics before Laura started to suspect something. It was the best way to avoid indiscreet questions.

'The food was delicious. We stayed there a couple of hours and then we left to go to bed an hour before the Darkening. I missed you, you know?'

These last words struck Andrea, who had never imagined he could strike Laura's soul like that. Strange, in a world where it was rare to have a steady girl or boy friend, it was just as strange to see a young woman like Laura choosing just one man. Perhaps it was just his impression, but thinking on it, even Andrea couldn't explain why he had chosen Laura that Saturday evening. A need to relax, maybe, or was he looking for love, seeing as his last relationship was six months ago. Hard to say. Maybe there wasn't a proper answer just like there wasn't an explanation for what had happened during that turbulent week; there really wasn't anything to explain, the most important thing was face the new way of seeing reality and Andrea realised the wisest thing to do was not to it alone.

So the phone call changed course suddenly.

'Me too!' answered Andrea almost automatically. 'Listen Laura, are you busy today at all?'

'No, it's my day off. Why?'

'Would you like to meet up?'

Andrea's voice had regained strength and frankness. The young Milanese knew what he wanted and how to get it.

'Of course, I really would like that. When?'

'Afternoon. Let's say at the Public Gardens at three, under the statue of the Misanthropic Angel. Is that alright?'

'OK then. I'll be there.'

The two said goodbye and the connection between the two mobiles ended. Andrea would have liked to end the call less abruptly, maybe by adding something tender but he couldn't come up with the right thing on the spur of the moment. He stood there still looking down at the floor, at the completely destroyed mains unit, and considered his situation. He thought back to the words just exchanged. 'Me too!'. New words for a world full of 'I', especially since Andrea had lost the pleasure of company. He had dramatically wasted a great opportunity last night; he was now in limbo wavering from one side to another, between company and the old man and the words 'me too' seemed to get him into gear and stop that endless swaying. 'Me too'. That is what she said, or something inside her had made her say it, but she had said it, and the person she had said it to could have found it useful, useful for his own aims. The clock struck ten past nine a.m. The date was at three in the afternoon. He still had time at his disposal but without any electricity the possibility to do something was limited. What could he do until three? Naturally, he would have thought and reflected, he would have counted the losses and the damage done because that morning he had woken up feeling wiser and sadder.

The rain came down fine but heavy. Out of the grey sky came the drops which fell gracefully onto the empty streets forming an invisible halo over every surface like a mystic presence that wrapped itself around the metallic shapes of the *transport*. Andrea who had just left his apartment to go to the appointment, had never dared to walk for a long time in the rain but now his old habits were a thing of the past. Now he only had to let himself go in a carefree fashion and ignore the fleeting passage of material things and think about their indefinite consistency. He thought mainly about how to act toward Laura. He would be meeting her soon now, and since this pretty red haired girl had kindled a new feeling in him, Andrea hadn't stopped feeling surprised. A different feeling, particular, out of the ordinary, what an emotion! Something deep and mysterious had kindled an intense throb in his heart and he felt like telling the world about it, like telling the people how he felt. Someone from the external world had to know about what he had experienced, it was the only way to be sure that he wasn't in error. At first Andrea decided against it but then it was impossible to ignore the fact that Laura could be the most suitable person. But how could he transmit this message? He thought about the old man and his methods but Andrea didn't think he was capable of imitating him. He didn't have a copy of 'The Divine Comedy' at hand. He could take his famous diary and maybe let Laura read his poem but he wondered what her reaction might be. Fear of being mocked or misunderstood haunted him. He felt embarrassed, embarrassed to show his personal work to a stranger. Why had he thought of the diary which was the source of so many complications and sufferance? And what if Laura didn't share his views? Would he run the risk of being teased or even rejected? This was an important occasion, a possibility not to be wasted. The diary meant danger but at the same time it was his only chance at success or escape. Maybe it was worth showing it. After all wasn't it the old man who said that the seal of freedom meant not being embarrassed at oneself? This flow of thoughts accompanied Andrea for the whole afternoon. He didn't hear the thunder echoing in the distance, he didn't even see the *transports* pass close by him, he could only hear the magic sound of the rain. Rain. The stuff that falls on the streets and flows down drains, the stuff that falls on our head and is drained away by a shower of thoughts.

Thinking. Thinking. Andrea suddenly found himself in front of the northern entrance of the Public Gardens. He had come quite a way, almost an hour's walk but he hadn't noticed the distance nor had he felt tired. It seemed to have faded as time passed. He went through the enormous arch and entered the immense green paradise of Milan. The Public Gardens stretched eastward as far as Piazza Babila covering an area of twenty square kilometres, almost the sum of the four *iperco-ops* put together. There weren't just lawns and lakes covering the surface but also sports fields, swimming pools, amusement parks, a zoo, and even some state of the art monuments here and there, at the crossroads, along the main path, around the fountains. Andrea went past some. They had twisted shapes which blended with the black of the metal, abstract shapes, incomprehensible, where it wasn't possible to recognise a human face, an expression or a desperate intertwining. Andrea stopped gazing and took the large path parallel to the perimeter park wall. There were a lot of people around despite the wet day. This place was never empty just like the CRS and that was obviously so because it was a Global Corp. decided for the citizens. Andrea however preferred to have no-one around him in such a delicate moment. The Misanthropic Angel was the only monument situated far away from the main paths and it had probably had no more than ten visitors ever since it had been erected. Hidden behind a thick foliage of a big hedge, Andrea had discovered it when he was a child during a visit to the zoo. He liked it straightaway because he could be alone there, aloof; it was a first approach to the world of solitude which he had come to know now at the age of thirty five. In that position where the Global Corp. sun never shone, the angel was a solitary figure, just like Andrea and it was precisely this that fascinated this young Milanese. Andrea had purposely arrived early and while waiting for Laura he sat on a wooden bench to carefully admire the marble statue, scratched with the effects of time but still sturdy on its pedestal with its sword held up toward the grey sky. He wondered what kind of life he had led and what he had felt, how many people had confided in it, how many things had happened in contact with its cold, smooth surface. Andrea imagined the old man sitting there in his place with his rusty gun in his hand and the bombs exploding in the nearby streets. He imagined his face looking much younger turned toward the Misanthropic Angel, his words imploring help, his conscience still undecided whether to fight or hide and he heard the rain falling on the damp ground, the shouts, the laughter and the deceit. Maybe this angel hadn't heard anything, hadn't felt anything that made it laugh. It was standing there holding up the weight of its years in absolute indifference, and Andrea hadn't noticed that while he was imagining all of this, time had passed, the world had changed and he was no longer the little boy at the zoo but the statue was still exactly the same.

'Hi!

Laura's whisper made Andrea was present again. He hadn't had time to consider what was happening around the statue. Fortunately the girl wasn't aware of his usual mind wandering and as soon as he said hello she moved toward him. Under her green umbrella she was as beautiful as ever. She was wearing a woollen pullover and a pair of dark trousers. This time her hair wasn't hanging down her shoulders but tied up into a lovely pony tail with a blue band. Andrea could stroke her hair as soon as she lay her head on his shoulder. How soft! Here, this is the image he should forever keep with him. Live without the slightest care in the world, without torment or fear, live quietly on this bench together with his angel. But Andrea had refused all that, he had let it slide away slowly so that now nothing was left. Sitting still on that bench he was aware he had lost something and when Laura lifted her head to talk to him he suddenly realised that nothing would ever be the same again, that things were moving to an end, toward nothingness. It had stopped raining now but a greyness still remained inside Andrea.

'Couldn't you have chosen another place to meet? For example, the Arch of Triumph?'

Laura looked around, lost. Her voice was trembling, maybe due to the cold or maybe she was afraid of the emptiness of that place, that silent and dark place with the pale face of the statue which was so unkempt and distressing.

'I don't you like solid, compact art forms that haven't got a definite shape; they are alienating. This is the only one I can identify myself with.'

Andrea nodded at Misanthropic Angel and Laura leered at him.

'But it's squalid!' said Laura with a whine. 'Look around you and tell me if you can see anything cheerful. I want to hear the twitter of little birds, I want to hear the warm chatter of people. I don't need this scary place to remind me what a grey day it is.'

'This is all quite beautiful…do you like the horizon?'

Andrea turned and his flash question caught Laura unprepared.

'What?' answered Laura.

'Do you like then horizon?" repeated Andrea.

'Yes, I like the horizon. So what?'

'Have you ever seen it?'

'Sometimes. It's over the skyscrapers where it's always been.'

'I know, but even if you can't see the horizon, it doesn't mean it doesn't exist in your heart.'

'What do you mean?'

'Nothing.'

Andrea's gaze returned to observe the statue and it seemed as if there were a smile on its face, an imperceptible smile. Andrea realised he had nothing to lose along the way and knowing it he felt a kind of pleasure. In his apparently disconnected discourses he felt as if he was close to something wonderful, more wonderful than anything else on earth. It was the same sentiment that primordial man had felt when he left his cavern for the first time and he saw the sun rising. It was the same light of hope and firmness. Gratitude, that's what it was. Gratitude for existing.

'Laura…'

Andrea took hold of the girl's hands and put them on his chest. He stared into her large anxious eyes and took a deep breath before continuing.

'It's as if…as if I was more myself when I'm in this place. More on my own, do you understand what I mean? I don't want to be just a cell in the body of society, I prefer to be something else.'

'Global Corp. is the saviour from chaos.' said Laura with a calm automatism. 'We can't live without the others or without Global Corp. which has worked things out so that we can all have our share of well-being. Thanks to this I have everything I need and I am free to enjoy my life in the best way possible. Nowadays everyone is happy.'

'But wouldn't you like to be free and be happy in another way, Laura? In your own way, for example and not in the way imposed on you by someone else? I want to know what real passion is, I want to feel something strongly, intensely, and not a mere artificial pleasure. It would be enough for me to make this old statue shine with a couple of cloths and bring back its original splendour in your honour. Wouldn't it be nice?'

'That isn't necessary. There are the robot-guardians for this kind of duty.'

'Of course it isn't necessary, but menial, humble work done nobly makes man worthy. I would like to do something worthy for you Laura, don't you understand?'

'But if there are the robot –guardians…'

'That's not the point!'

'Have you gone mad, Andrea?'

'No, I'm not mad. The fact is I would do all this because…'

'Because…?'

Laura expected an answer and Andrea was fed up of making things up; he didn't want to diminish the power of his spirit just to cover things up. He suddenly felt as if his spirit was bubbling awake. That was a sign, a sign telling him he had reached the climax, the right moment when everything would come together in perfect harmony. Andrea didn't hesitate, he just let himself go and gave in to the impetus of his spirit just as he did over the diary a few days beforehand.

'Because…?' repeated Laura.

'….because I love you!' exclaimed Andrea.

The phrase came out clear and distinct from his lips. He kept his gaze upon Laura and in pronouncing those three words he felt a kind of thrill come over his body. That thrill was more than a simple neurochemical reaction to his body, but rather a supernatural sensation that had finally made his weary body feel alive. It had been wonderful to let his subconscious speak, it had been sublime to feel full of gratitude and beauty, and the most beautiful thing of all was that there was no 'why' to answer. Andrea had realised he had the capability to surprise himself and believing in himself had given him a sense to life.

'Are you serious?' reacted Laura smiling and hugging him closely.

'Well…really…'

Andrea felt a sudden uneasiness. That wasn't what he really meant. It was something even bigger going beyond any barrier; it wasn't just love but a lot of things rolled into one which enhanced human spirit. However, Laura hadn't grasped the concept and Andrea realised that the words spoken did not sound like that special thing he had expected.

'Silly!' said Laura in a childish voice. 'Don't make too many problems out of it. You know I want you. And if you want me too why all this story? Come on, let's go to your place!'

This time Laura's sensual proposal annoyed the young Milanese. Andrea let go of her affectionate cuddle and looking at her seriously he pointed an accusing finger at her.

'Do you always have to think of only one thing?' scolded Andrea. 'In this world everyone just thinks about their own pleasure each one according to their own needs. It's an indecent orgy. There is much more above this lustful and material life, don't you realise?'

'But everyone's doing it...' answered Laura intimidated.

'Well done!' replied Andrea. 'Follow everyone and do what everyone else does! You know what I say? You're a little useless and pathetic woman...'

'But how...' stuttered Laura as she tasted sweetness turning sour.

'...a blonde bimbo that doesn't understand a thing...' continued Andrea.

'Stop!' begged Laura.

'...a nice little bite of flesh to tear apart and split up to satisfy every pleasure...' Andrea hammered on again.

'Enough...stop...' begged Laura again.

Her pleads were lost between the sighs of her weeping. Andrea's claims were full of indignation and evilness but they were especially scathing on the helpless skin of the young girl. She had always believed in satisfaction through pleasure and uncontrolled enjoyment to lead a happy life, she couldn't hold back the tears in the throes of pain. She couldn't stand the cruelty that had been thrown in her face by Andrea. Those notes of reproach were overwhelming, unbearable and as cold as marble.

'You're just like the others.' added Andrea in a despising tone. 'You're just nobody!'

He jumped up and without saying another word he went off, leaving Laura sitting alone on the bench. Alone, alone with the Misanthropic Angel, who had listened to the conversation in silence. Except for the statue no-one could hear her cries as she tried to calm down or see her tears fall onto dry, smooth cheeks. No-one could hear her quiet weeping. Laura didn't want anyone to hear her. Nowadays everyone is happy, thought Laura to herself. I have everything I need. There's no need to feel sad. Just a few words to calm herself down and the bad moment was already a thing of the past, already forgotten. She took a handkerchief from her pocket, delicately dried her eyes and looked around her, then she got up from the bench to start looking for some form of fun. That was the end of Andrea and Laura's affair.

Andrea had already gone through the northern arch and was walking thoughtlessly along the external wall of the Public Gardens. The determined man of a few minutes ago no longer existed. He was nervous. He had gone back to being the man hit by remorse, an even more excruciating remorse that was impossible to ignore. Why had he behaved like that? What sense was there in making poor Laura feel so desperate? Her candid cheeks spoiled by those drops of salty water! What a shame! On second thoughts Andrea felt ashamed. He had shown how capable he could be, but at a price. He saw himself to be like the old man, doing the same things with the same moralising tone but he hadn't been at all calm or reflexive or patient like the old man. On the contrary, he had been so violent that he scared himself, he had unintentionally revealed the negative side of his dark subconscious, and it was his own fault if he had destroyed his central mains unit and he had also lost his beautiful Laura. And what for? To satisfy his conceit, that's why, to become that longed for 'individual' which at the end was imperfect and unbalanced. Andrea admitted he had done it all wrong but there was no way he could turn back on his steps. He had decided to fly beyond the boundaries of the sky to get some satisfaction but he had flown far too high and he lost sight of the earth beneath his feet, he had lost sight of the roofs of the buildings, the faces of the people and he was alone. He had rejected Laura, he had let Marco disappear again, he had kept Alberoni at a distance and all the rest. There was nobody else. So Andrea would now go back to the crypt to talk to the old man, to say sorry to tell him he still needed him. He had been selfish, impulsive, ungrateful, uncaring, he had learnt his lesson and now he was ready to get back into the right lane that he had arbitrarily changed. The old man was his only way out.

Andrea walked the whole of the north-west perimeter wall of the Public Gardens until he came to the Laurent-Chanel building. The clouds continued to get thicker and soon it would start raining again. Andrea hadn't thought about the past for some time and wasn't really interested in the grey day reflected on the splendid windows of the Laurent-Chanel. He saw his silhouette in the glass of the automatic doors and how he split up as the doors opened wide. He went into the *iperco-op* slowly, making for the moving walkway. He stood weak and limp on it, rather like the living dead, but Andrea wasn't really bothered. Being among so many dead who were laughing, shopping, selling or eating didn't feel at all uncomfortable. It was sufficient for him to know he was different, he was the only one with an active mind inside that modest skull. He gazed around half dazed and peered at the bad copies of men making exaggerated purchases, commenting on the Autumn shades of their clothes, chatting about the latest novelty at the CRS, keeping in touch with old friends and making fun of their jokes, watching a match at the Public Gardens, ordering a juicy beef T-bone steak at the Steak House, go training regularly in the gym (three times a week), going and coming, taking this and that, going and coming back, sleeping well (no more bad dreams), eating well (less fat and GMOs), not drinking too much, no excesses, no possibility to escape, walking at a well-kept pace, calm, attending the meeting with the CEO, applauding the President of the Global Corp., getting on with ones' work mates, regularly checking one's Net-Bank code, having a peaceful soul (no paranoia), being part of the informed society, involved but without power, keen but not in love, that does not cry in public, that does not get carried away at the virtual cinema, that kisses with saliva, being a man who is no longer empty and frantic but healthier, happier, more productive and able to laugh at other people's weaknesses, to smile and forget what we were smiling about only to smile again…

These people had no sense of direction; they moved in a disorderly fashion in a space without time or memory. Andrea however was no longer one of them. Behind this claim he felt a bitter after taste because he wasn't one of them anymore, but he had left the world of dreams to wake up in a crude and sad reality where time was ruthless in marking his heartbeats. Andrea couldn't forget his memories of the past. He particularly remembered Laura's face, in tears, and now he only felt remorse. Damned remorse. The others didn't have these sentiments for the simple fact that they had never dared to be pitiless against others. Andrea had, on the other hand, behaved like a monster whose actions were unforgivable.

Meanwhile the moving walkway had carried him on to the end of the main corridor toward the future. Andrea put his sadness to one side in the hope that a more glorious future awaited him, and between one display unit of oriental perfumes and a shop of chic dresses, he passed through such a lovely yet ugly world. A see-saw world, full of contradictions that out of irony of fate led him to the old man's shelter.

At the beginning of the alley there was the street cleaning machine but not a soul about. Andrea retraced those memorable steps in his mind and remembered the start of the whole issue. He remembered running away from the police, hiding behind the street cleaning machine, the cat, the dark, when he discovered the hole cover and the encounter with the old man. It was a meeting which happened by chance but seemed to have a precise aim for Andrea: to find himself. Perhaps this was the desire of his subconscious. He walked those few metres full of hope and slipped into the hole another time. As soon as he was inside a flash of thunder sounded in the sky and it started pouring down. The corridor inside was colder and darker than usual. The light at the end of the corridor was dimmer in intensity and Andrea couldn't see the end of the corridor. The young Milanese took a few steps forward and when he reached the threshold the scene in front of him was quite unexpected. The room had been turned upside down. Most of the candles had been thrown on the floor just like the heavy books scattered here, there and everywhere. The furniture too was out of place, the wardrobe wide open, the desk upside down, it looked as if a tornado had hit the place. And there on the floor buried under hundreds of pieces of paper lay the old man's body. Andrea first thought he was just sleeping and he shook him a couple of times. No answer. He shook him again. No low moans, no answer. He couldn't imagine he was faced with a dead body, he couldn't believe he was facing the scourge Global Corp. that had always kept hidden in the far off *gerials*. He shook him again and with all his strength he pulled him out of that mountain of paper. He was lying stomach down with one arm parallel to his body and the other turned toward his desk. Andrea didn't understand. He decided to turn him round with his stomach facing up. But as he did so, he saw death in the face for the first time in his life, he saw death looking at him straight in the eye with an empty, indifferent gaze. His face was pale, very pale and cold, very cold. His facial features were rigid and still, as they were the moment life had been taken away. His mouth was wide open. For Andrea it was a moment of panic, a tremendous shock which made him jump back against the cold, hard wall. He let out a gasp but then put his hand over his mouth so as not to desecrate the silence of that place. Sitting with his back against the wall he observed the old man whose head was slightly inclined toward Andrea looking at him now with a mixture of anguish and a serenity. Andrea wanted to look away.

'My God...' he whispered clenching his teeth. 'My God...'

In that moment of pain and regret which filled his head, the only word which came out was 'God'. A word quite alien to him but he kept repeating it spontaneously and convincingly. If this God really existed he would give him the strength to overcome feelings of guilt. The old man was dead because of him and Andrea couldn't accept the idea that he would have to drag this burden of remorse on his shoulders. He couldn't stand that accusing and obsessive gaze of the old man. Yet both of his glassy eyes continued to shine a light and it was these two gems set in their sockets that encouraged Andrea to tell himself that the old man's spirit lived on and he didn't blame him for anything. Andrea magically calmed down and as soon as the panic had gone he stayed to watch over the old man, trying to imagine that moment, that swift visit of death.

...The old man's heart had stopped beating, his voice had made its last breath, his mouth open as if making a last effort to fill his lungs with air. But it was as if he had forgotten how to breathe. He moved his arms flying about here and there, trying to shout out but not a sound came out; only the terror in his eyes revealed what he was going through. He put his hands to his throat, grabbing at the air, the air he could no longer breathe, the air which no longer existed for him.

Death. Here it was, before his very eyes. What a strange phenomenon, thought Andrea. Indeed, both for him and any citizen of Global Corp. death wasn't that big thing to be afraid of. The Global Corp. had made things so that it didn't exist in the heart and minds of happy people. This only increased Andrea's hate of the lying society and he felt betrayed, exploited and seeing the old man dead could only make him feel grief and anger. Grief and anger. He felt that jerking thrill inside him and his soul was filled with it. His spirit, his subconscious, or whatever it was, announced that he would soon wake up and he would have declared revenge, a tremendous revenge. Andrea smiled maliciously, satisfied, determined. He took his gaze away from the old man's face and looked at the rest of his body and remembered his arm turned toward the desk. The old man's hand was leaning on a greyish sheet of paper different from all the other pieces and he was holding a goose feather between his fingers. There was some writing on the page while the tip of the feather was stained black. Andrea realised that the old man had wanted to write something on the point of death. He moved closer, took the sheet and began reading the wobbly lines.

Then made reply: "A conscience overcast
Or with its own or with another's shame,
Will taste forsooth the tartness of thy word;

But ne'ertheless, all falsehood laid aside,
Make manifest thy vision utterly,
And let them scratch wherever is the itch;

For if thine utterance shall offensive be
At the first taste, a vital nutriment
'Twill leave thereafter, when it is digested.

This cry of thine shall do as doth the wind,
Which smiteth most the most exalted summits,
And that is no slight argument of honour.

The lines instilled confidence in Andrea just as they had done when he had read his composition in the diary. It was another of Dante's quotation. Probably the old man had left this message especially for him; another gesture of goodwill. It was Andrea's mission to follow those words. He couldn't fully understand what was written but he knew which road he was meant to follow. That road sometimes loved, sometimes hated. Andrea had been offered another opportunity not to be missed. He would have put his self-pity to one side and he would have come forward in honour of Laura and Marco; he would have climbed the highest peak in honour of then old man. Andrea suddenly felt much more confident, and in dreaming success, the paper slipped out of his hand falling reversed onto the carpet of papers. On the other side of the sheet there was another piece of writing and Andrea moved closer out of curiosity and excitement to read it.

I will accept a quiet life, a hand shake, some carbon monoxide without any alarm or surprise.

R.

This sentence didn't seem to make much sense. Maybe it was something separate which had nothing to do with the Dante's verses. Why worry about it? Dante was a more reliable source; the road was already open, all he had to do was follow it bravely and quickly. Andrea let the page fall a second time, on purpose this time, then he got up and looked around him. He had never seen the room so dark before. The number of candles lit were now only two here and there in the dark and Andrea's eyes fell onto something glittering at the feet of the desk. The young Milanese recognised the gun that the old man had used to attack him some time ago. The gun. It wasn't just a souvenir, it was a weapon of defence just in case.

Andrea bent down to pick it up but as he did so there was cold wind from behind which blocked him. The black veil of death seemed to have brushed close by him and suddenly brought a shadow of fear over him. It was a warning; death was always behind the corner waiting and one day or another it would have been his turn. The more he thought about it, the more frightened he became. He had to move quickly and knowing that death lived in the uncertainty of the future he realised he had to seek the past as his best fixed point.

The clock in one of the many McDonald-Nestlé shops was out of order and even if it said the wrong time no-one seemed particularly bothered. Andrea was sitting at a table without ordering anything and without any expression on his face he observed the people enjoying huge quantities of food just as if they were stuffing their brains with useless data. Andrea was disgusted by it all. He was disgusted by the way, right from the start, he had been deceived. He was about to jump up when a voice whispered something in his head.
'Careful, consider the situation and then decide what to do.'
Enough! Andrea wanted to disobey that cautious and wise voice, he wanted to play in a dangerous way for a change, to stop the uniform way he lived his boring life without any genuine vitality. He took the gun from out of his suede jacket pocket, he raised it to man's height and in a flash he let out all his anger. He fired the first two shots by chance and suddenly patches of blood appeared on the pale green walls. He fired more shots and all his victims stared at him with a flat, empty, almost melancholic expression. The bullets drove into their thick stupidity and they seemed unable to react. In the meantime the alarm had gone off and Andrea absorbed by the devastating justice didn't hear the police breaking into the place. A

shot in the back of his head came quickly and Andrea fell to the ground before being able to finish his round of bullets. The alarm stopped immediately and the young Milanese slipped again into total darkness. Into darkness.

IX

Andrea opened his eyes gently. The surroundings slowly began to take shape. First they were a mixed up mass of colour and then came more shapes and neater outlines, and gradually, as soon as his eyes were used to the light, Andrea realised where he was. It was a large room with two large floor-to-ceiling windows. The curtains had been drawn but the light of day penetrated rather intensely and the young Milanese realised he must have slept at least until late morning. The walls were a sea blue and next to the comfortable sea blue couch on which Andrea was lying, there was a large aquarium full of multicolour and multiform fish. The rest of the house was furnished with a wide range of interesting furniture and ornaments. In the middle of the room there was a small white coffee table decorated with shells and flowers; on the right there were some statues from the classical age including two thick Doric columns placed at the sides of a private lift. On the walls there were large and small frames portraying views of Milan and other international cities while large screens hung in every corner, even on the ceiling, gave out the latest breaking news non-stop, accompanied by lively silent images. In the background there was a continuous playback at low volume of the sound of a flock of seabirds and the rolling waves of a rough sea, a marine melody which created the atmosphere of peace and quiet as well as being in line with the chromatic colours of the room. This certainly wasn't Andrea's room nor was it the room of an ordinary Global Corp. citizen. It was a much bigger room than expected, maybe it was just a part of a much bigger floor. Where on earth could he be? Memory of the previous night's movements were still a bit confused; however he hadn't forgotten the blows of the cosh which had left its signs, a large bump and an annoying headache. He tried to get up slowly without making any jerky movements so he could get into a sitting position when his eyes fell onto the end of the room where there was a big desk and some large shelves which could not be missed. Andrea was especially struck by the shelves. They were similar, very similar to the shelves belonging to the old man except that instead of books on them there was a series of mini discs and CD–ROMs. Between the two shelves, in the middle of the wall, there was a large portrait hanging majestically with a sign and some cubital writing on it.

COMMUNITY – IDENTITY – STABILITY

Andrea memorised the words then looked again at the portrait. It was the portrait of a man of about fifty, clean shaven, dressed smart, with a radiant smile and an assuring look. The fair colouring of his face on a dark background highlighted a well-known face to Andrea, but before he could say a word the lift doors opened behind him.

'Good morning, Mr Rossi!'

A man with a smiling face came out of the lift. He was well dressed in a grey suit and Bordeaux tie. It was the same man as the one in the portrait wearing the same suit.

'I'm pleased you have come round…I was afraid the blow you got was a bit too strong. Do you feel more at ease this morning?'

Andrea kept silent with his mouth gaping. He wasn't sure how to react in front of this man who was the most important man in the world, the President of Global Corp.

'Surprised eh?' he continued walking toward the opposite side of the room. 'Well who wouldn't be? It isn't every day that you get to be in front of the Big Chief in person!

The man smiled again and sat behind his desk. Andrea had got up slowly, still uncertain about how to behave, and walked to the middle of the room.

'Don't be scared!' the President said in a friendly tone. 'Take a seat!'

The President pointed to a chair in front of the desk and Andrea sat down right away. He had the President of Global Corp in front of him but still couldn't grasp what was happening.

'Where are we?' asked Andrea in a low voice.

'We're on the top floor of the Cedir.' answered the President making himself comfortable on his chair. 'Please excuse the curtains but I haven't had time to tidy the place. I arrived this morning from New York and I thought the central unit had been programmed. Did you have a sweet awakening?'

'I think so.' muttered Andrea a bit confused by it all.

'You look confused. I bet you've got a lot of questions for me, haven't you?'

His voice was calm, welcoming. Andrea sensed something strange. He could remember everything that had happened, the havoc he had caused but he couldn't understand how come he had ended up at the Cedir in front of the President of Global Corp.

'Well...President...'

'My name is Henry Branson. The term "President" can be left for the others.'

President Branson made a gesture with his hand as if to mean the rest of the world population outside those walls; it was as if they were the only two who existed and he clearly noticed how the P resident was slightly curious to know this man standing before him, who had brought chaos to the quiet Milanese life.

'Well, Mr. Branson...'

Andrea couldn't help stammering. He was finally face to face with the man who would have listened to his voice, if only he could put a string of words together. The questions wouldn't come and the only thing coming out of his mouth was a mutter.

'I see you don't know where to start. So, I'll start then, shall I? I must say I am surprised, if not shocked by your behaviour. Last night, when we got the news at the Congress, no-one was expecting it, least of all me. Fortunately the place was almost empty when the Milan police came and managed to curb the extent of the incident. The victims died instantly. Just as well that there were only about fifteen witnesses all in shock, otherwise now panic would be raging everywhere. There was the risk of a total crisis. At this point, however, I don't feel any wrath toward you, on the contrary, you arouse my curiosity and it isn't the first time either. Your behaviour has already aroused suspicion in a group of undercover policemen. At the beginning their ambush seemed unjustified and anti-establishment. But I soon realised that they weren't completely wrong…'

Andrea thought back to the incident of two weeks ago. So much time had passed since then but he could remember exactly what the aggressors had said. 'And you, idiot, who said he was an old fashioned type!'. He now realised what they had meant. That also explained the unexpected police alarm and the boy's fear after being attacked in the street. In the Darkening he hadn't been able to see the faces of his aggressors; how could he be sure that boy was one of them? Only because he had recognised his shaven head in the moment of rage? The old man was right: the history of the Men of the Night was a pure invention.

'…A few days ago I was informed by the CEO of the Compagnia of a similar case analysed by the Knowledgeer. The computer had come up with bizarre results almost as if it wasn't capable of scanning your cerebral profile. So I advised the CEO to keep an eye on things and we were able to get into action before you carried out a massacre.'

'How? By using spies?' asked Andrea mentally referring to the presumed stalker with the dark Ray Ban glasses.

'Nothing like that Mr. Rossi.' Branson denied categorically. 'We are not at war. We are not enemies. It is the normal safety procedure carried out thanks to our efficient satellite system. Your fantasy is running away with you, don't you think?'

'I'm different from you, Mr. Branson.' answered Andrea in a challenging tone. 'I don't spy on people, I don't follow and copy what everyone else does and above all I don't let people treat me like a robot.'

Andrea had got hold of the situation. He didn't intend to feel any sense of guilt. This was the moment he had been waiting for and this first comment was only the beginning. Once the conversation had got going he would have got into gear and he would have discovered the truth from the man who himself filtered the truth.

'You make me more and more curious, Mr. Rossi,' said Branson straightening his jacket and resting his elbows on the desk. 'I have never seen any citizen get so agitated like this. I must say your statements really do surprise me. Not to mention that precious object you were carrying with you.'

President Branson opened a small casket on his right and took out Andrea's killer gun. Andrea didn't even look at it, neither did he say a word. He knew perfectly why his behaviour appeared so ambiguous. No quiet citizen of Global Corp. would have ever dared to be different from the others, no-one in the world would have ever protested or disowned this well-off society they lived in. But Andrea's spirit had become peculiar. Just the simple fact that the Knowledgeer hadn't been able to interpret

Andrea's feelings explained his every diversity and this was his invitation card into President Branson's office.

'A great piece of antiquity!' replied Branson. 'They are no longer in circulation. It's a pity they are a thing of the past!'

'And what do you mean by that? Why refuse the past? Why allow the past to be corrupted or even suppressed?'

'Because it's all old stuff, Mr. Rossi. It makes our progress heavy and slows us down needlessly. Man's world is so old that all of its past history can't be kept. Everything has to be selected and it has to follow the requirements of Global Corp. otherwise…'

'But you haven't got the right to destroy the past! It contains so many wonderful things. Dante, for example?'

'The poet from Florence? The journey beyond the grave? Intriguing! "Midway upon the journey of our life…". It's one of my favourite readings!'

'You mean you've read Dante too?' exclaimed Andrea surprised.

'Of course,' answered Branson getting up from his chair. 'And lots of other things.'

In saying that he got up and went over to the portrait. Behind the painting there was a wall safe. President Branson placed his hand on a print detector and the security door sprung open. Inside there were some papers, just like the ones the old man had, and also a couple of books with dark brown covers. Andrea gave a quick glance as the door shut. President Branson took the books and lay them on the desk. Andrea read the titles: 'The Divine Comedy', 'Romeo and Juliet', 'The Bible'. He was amazed to see that the President of Global Corp. had cultivated such a passion for reading and writing.

'I wonder how you have managed to read stuff like this, Mr. Rossi. In Global Corp.'s early years these books were prohibited, then they disappeared completely, leaving space for poor imitations which do respect Global Corp.'s way of thinking.'

Andrea smirked. The old man's hiding place hadn't been discovered. The satellite hadn't been precise enough to report an abandoned alley way near Piazza Agostino. Andrea had no intention of revealing this piece of information or his source, he wanted it to remain a mystery so as to have an advantage over a smart person like President Branson.

'Why have you deprived everyone of such wisdom?'

'For the simple fact that we don't know what to do with old stuff. Our world isn't like Dante's or Shakespeare's.'

'It's your fault!'

'Civilisation is to blame. Old things are not compatible with medicine and technology. Our civilisation has chosen progress and has had to put books to one side. Indeed, I keep these books hidden in the safe, because if they were read these days, they would upset anyone, putting the peace of our community at risk. Naturally, it's Global Corp.'s duty to check and revise via the Opsolector every form of reading that may go against its requirements. Anyway, people today haven't time to read and understand, maybe they can manage a summary or review in an electronic magazine. As you, can see we don't need the past anymore!'

'Perhaps old things can be cancelled without leaving any trace but man too gets old.'

'That's why we have *gerials*. The old and static society doesn't think about young people. For this reason we keep old people far away from our cities to avoid them influencing the ongoing modernisation of Global Corp. I myself am forty-nine years old and in eleven years' time I'll have to leave my position to my successor. It isn't just a matter of progress but it's also a question of balance within our society. Old age is an illness. Gradually, as we get older, passions appease and pleasures are less stimulating; our reasoning makes its role perfect and it is no longer deceived by images or desires and distractions we used to be absorbed by. So the old man stops to think and reflect and easily feels the wind of time which inevitably passes. Time is the present, or rather, that short moment which separates the past from the future. But if the past no longer exists and the future isn't here yet, how can Time exist as a separation between two entities that don't exist? When it is necessary to recognise if one is happy, at the precise moment when you ask yourself that question well, we let's be truthful, not everyone is capable of doing it. This is the damage caused by history. When an individual is feeling at the mercy of the past, he feels a sense of impotence towards the present, losing trust in the chance to shape his or her future. Global Corp. aims to crystallise Time, eliminate the past and reduce man's memory to an infinite present without a first and a later. Exclude a man from the flow of time and he will stop suffering. A bit like those fish.'

President Branson pointed to the aquarium.

'Fish have a short memory of about two or three minutes and they have to swim without ever stopping to live because if they stop they die. In the same way an individual who thinks too much of his memories, his hopes or problems or death, will end up living in anxiety. This sufferance involves a greyness to their existence and in the chaos of real life God becomes the only means of defence. Do you know who God is?'

'I have heard of Him.' answered Andrea vaguely.

'I expected an answer like that seeing as you've read "The Divine Comedy"... Anyway, as I was saying, God rises up from behind the clouds and our souls turn to that source of light, because the vital rush which characterises the world of sensations, has started to fade; we feel the need to lean against something which won't play a nasty trick on us, an absolute and eternal truth. The concept of end is an illusory idea that can easily condition the individual, and Global Corp. cannot allow itself to disturb the quiet life of the community. Indeed, the individual, believing the solution to everything lies in something beyond our senses, beyond the human sphere, would lose his faith in the Supreme Welfare of the Global Corp. Actually, the aim of life doesn't lie in the purification of the conscience or in some extension of knowledge but in the maintaining of well-being.'

'But if man lives and breathes' interrupts Andrea. 'There must be a reason!'

'You can't come to any concrete conclusion asking why we exist.' reflected Branson. 'Man is a machine but he has difficulty in considering himself as such. He is nothing else but an element of a mechanic nature, and like machines, he turns on, feeds, wastes energy, turns off, and builds with the others a society without having to think about anything else. We smooth out the road so that an individual doesn't follow commitments, doesn't have responsibilities but lives his life moment by moment, without putting any burdens on his shoulders. On thinking too much, the individual would discover his state, he would suddenly understand the fault of the past and would follow an abstract and useless objective like God. The concept of end could be true but under the actual circumstances it is inadmissible. We no longer need God. Once people believed in God because they were overrun with wars, plagues, and evil of every kind. Today, people believe in the Global Corp. because they know they can have the guarantee of a quiet and peaceful life.'

President Branson finished his sentence and pressed a button on a panel placed between the casket and the hard drive on the desk. Suddenly the wall on Andrea's right began to move sideways and slowly revealed a giant *dvd-screen*. The President pressed another button and after a couple of voice commands the screen came on showing the main menu and several hyper textual links. The title was 'Universal Genetic Archives' and underneath a phrase flashed which was announcing the updating of embryo 2453839. A click here, a command there and a display showed the virtual figure of a man in perpetual rotation. Next to it there was a chart which explained in detail his name, surname, his Net-Bank code, his date of birth as well as his systemship date, his genetic code, his profession, his friends. In the section 'habits' a wide red band confirmed the reason for an update and Andrea felt strangely like a black beetle on a white carpet.

'The bio economy was started in 1953 when Francis Crick and James Watson identified the structure and double spiral of DNA. After more than a century organic biotechnology has outdated information technology and its inorganic materials, and today it is possible to scan biological processes.

First of all we have taken away from man and woman the right to procreate immeasurably. Every city of the world contains exactly five million people. Thanks to the bioengineering of Celera Genomics we are able to control the number of births and maintain the demographic growth at a constant level. Our eugenics policy has the objective to forge individuals with personalities and habits which remain within the limits required by Global Corp. We don't allow them to live in solitude but we encourage them to socialise. Once only four kinds of information could be manipulated: numbers, words, sounds and images. But information comes to us through smells, taste, imagination and intuition. We can now extend the field to these areas. This is how the son of our society is born and we proceed with a strict hypnopaedia which can be considered complete by the twentieth year of age. The individual is ready to be part of the system and from then on, until death, Global Corp. watches over him. The central computer of Cedir, present in every city, registers each and every movement, it follows the individual's behaviour, it looks after his health and checks his state of affluence. The most important thing is the digit-controlled healthcare; DNA and the individual's organism can be analysed straightaway and we are able to immediately recognise any kind of anomaly and intervene in time. This continuous health check-up reduces risks and expenses. The stabiliser lends an extra hand. They are biochemical pills or phials which sooth or stimulate certain chemical reactions in our organism, cancelling deterring effects like depression.

The same method is applied to OGM food which are prefabricated giving man the proteins he needs. A clear example is rice reinforced with beta carotene which our body converts into vitamin A and iron. This type of rice is an improved species and can't be found in nature. Together with many other genetically modified foods they correct nutritional values and are necessary to balance man's biological life and make it less risky. The same thing is valid in the workplace and social life. The individual receives an adequate E-credit from Global Corp. so they can make use of every kind of commodity; his predestined job is simple and tranquil, feasible within reasonable time. Global Corp. and the machines make everything easy. The individual lives in peace and quiet knowing that mother society protects him twenty four hours a day.'

'How dare you control the lives of people, who gives you that permission? Why don't you give people a moment of personal life?'

'Because everything that passes through one's own autonomy isn't accepted by the authorities. As you well know, I have the duty to maintain peace on the whole planet. Therefore the body of society must remain intact although the single cells can change.'

'This is a dictatorship, that's what it is!'

'Not at all! It is a simple security procedure inside our community. Circumstances force humanists to chase after scientific propaganda just like the liberal chases the dictator. Every form of order is better than chaos. There isn't a civilisation without social stability, there isn't social stability without individual stability.'

'What happens to the soul of the individual, the true essence of man? And the poetic spirit of Dante? Such uniqueness cannot be cancelled!'

'Global Corp. can't permit particularities within the community. Anyway, as for the poetic spirit I deeply admired your meticulous work.'

President Branson opened the casket where the gun had been kept, and showed him the diary with the red cover. Andrea stalled for an instant staring at his small secret in the hands of a stranger. They had managed to get hold of his diary. That meant they must have surely followed him in every one of his reflections in front of those pages, enough to appreciate the contents and be impressed by them. Andrea felt satisfied in that moment and didn't think in the slightest what could have happened later.

'A really good piece of work!' continued Branson showing acknowledgement as he put the diary back on the desk. 'Unfortunately I can't accept it! It is a highly harmful object. Its uniqueness could provoke disorder, havoc. Fortunately genetics allow us to project and develop human minds according to fixed rules in perfect harmony without any imbalances or anomalies.'

'You're destroying creativity, aren't you?'

'Not exactly. Creativity can also bring positive effects. In a certain sense we could say that automatism is a kind of controlled creativity. For example, the *beta tester* that programmes a software for the CRS by using a certain number of rules it recognises, has more freedom than the poet who writes whatever comes into his head and is slave to other rules which he is unaware of. Poets cloud their waters because this way they seem deeper and the writer sublimes his own restlessness by seriously upsetting others.'

'I know what you're trying to tell me.' said Andrea taking on a diplomatic tone. 'There's one thing that isn't clear to me, Mr. Branson. Up till now you've talked about how indispensable it is not to disturb the community, you've stressed several times the importance of normality against everything that is different. It's a matter of maintaining social stability but what is the advantage for the individual?'

Andrea asked himself this question with a veiled irony convinced he had left the President of Global Corp. in a checkmate position.

'Happiness, Mr. Rossi!' answered Branson crossing his legs and entwining his fingers on his knees. 'Man has always been looking for happiness and has had to live in anxiety to get it. Perhaps the actual happiness can appear artificial and squalid compared to the offset of sadness, but people don't pay much attention to it. No-one really knows what happiness is anyway and so it has to be standardised through all these reforms which we have partially mentioned previously. Obviously the result is the absolute best. Everything is for the better in the best of all possible worlds.'

'This isn't the best of possible worlds.'

'Will you give me a reason why it shouldn't be so?'

'Because...'

Andrea hesitated. It was difficult to talk about things that didn't have words to express them; the bird that perches on the window sill, a tree in spring, a tree in autumn, a small child running in the street, stone, concrete, plastic. Andrea would have liked to say something about the night, about shadows, about solitude and death. He would have liked to talk but there weren't the words to explain. Not even in Dante.

'You don't seem to be able to answer Mr. Rossi.' said Branson seeing Andrea in difficulty. 'Therefore I'll speak for you. You have to know that vegetative happiness is man's ignorance about his unhappy state of being. In order to have a good and prefect world we have had to destroy conscience and transform everything into vegetable without a will, but happy to enjoy a care free life.'

'You limit the freedom of each one of us like this!' replied Andrea coming back to his senses after being speechless.

'Freedom is a mirage!' exclaimed Branson. 'Man has never been free. He has always been slave to his prejudices and his character traits since the dawn of time. And freedom means pursuing one's own dreams in a higgledy-piggledy fashion without any control and at the end the disappointment of not seeing it coming true causes nothing but sufferance. The spirit of community help dominates life in our system: the individual is entrusted to Global Corp., embryo formation starts straightaway and then education. Knowledge imparted always has a social function and for us the best way to do it is to keep it superficial. Ignorance is strength. There is a lot of pain in knowing and those who broaden their own consciences also broaden their sadness. Centuries ago knowledge was a far more valuable asset, truth was a supreme value; but all the rest was second place and subordinated. Mass production required change. Universal happiness keeps gears in constant movement; beauty and truth can't do this. People were ready to have their desires controlled. Anything for a happy life. Happiness has its price. And it isn't just literature and art that are incompatible with the system at Global Corp.: science too is incompatible. Science is dangerous, a reward in itself, and when it is transgressive, it can generate monsters. Science at Global Corp. is a recipe book with an orthodox theory about cooking which no-one ever questions; it is a list of recipes that have to be added with the consent of the cook who in this case is me. As you can see Mr. Rossi everything is free and everything is compulsory.'

'It remains a dictatorship!'

'It isn't a dictatorship but a masked control aimed at supreme well-being. Global Corp. citizens are imprisoned, but aren't aware of their imprisonment. Orthodoxy is unconscious. Global Corp. runs in their blood, it's imprinted in their DNA.'

President Branson pointed to the screen as if to highlight yet again the advantage genetic engineering had brought them. Then he turned to Andrea again who had silently got up and moved toward the curtains of the nearest large window. He kept a fixed gaze trying to find among his thoughts another point he could discuss. It was absurd. Everything seemed to have a convincing line of argument yet this limiting behaviour of Global Corp. wasn't right toward his 'I'. He looked away a couple of times but when he moved them a second time he noticed a small picture hanging on the strip of wall between the two large windows. It was an old black and white sketch of Milan. There were the statues, the street lamps, an old building on the area where McDonald-Nestlé now stood, the old trams on the roads, the stalls. Andrea remembered the old man straightaway and with one thought he commemorated his patriotism of past times. He let out an inaudible sigh and, without turning, asked his next question.

'Besides individual freedom,' asked Andrea. 'You've also swept away the political freedom of whole nations, haven't you?'

'As I've just said,' answered Branson. 'Civilisation has absolutely no need for nobility of soul or heroism.

The vital dash of the individual isn't necessary, but community spirit is. Global Corp. is very careful about preventing someone from loving something else too much. There's nothing worse than a divided or split obedience. Nations were the symbol of this fragmentation and their diversity and conflicts had always hindered the progress of world co-operation. In fact over the centuries there have always been wars fighting for their own interests, especially power and wealth. One part of the world didn't seem to understand what pleases another and the continuous friction only seemed to worsen the situation. Thus, the idea to establish a substantial equality among everyone came up, no longer having races any more, nor religions, social class, different traditions or mentalities. A long time ago it was thought that this was an unfeasible utopia but the solution was soon found thanks to the miracle of Celera Genomics: since families generated men of different factions it was necessary to give birth to individuals from the same womb, from the mother society of Global Corp. and make them all equal. This way the vision of the world became homogeneous and identical for each individual. At the beginning all attempts failed but when genetic mapping became fully available and Global Corp. obtained definite and total control of births, unification of opposites finally came about and a millenary desire came true: world peace.'

'And all the people who have ethnic origin, language and traditions in common?' asked Andrea repeating the definition of a nation.

'That's old stuff too!' repeated Branson rather fed up of the continuous repetition. 'A patriot is out of fashion these days with his machine gun and his speeches about the strength of a nation. There are no longer any nations. Planes fly freely over us and data bits flow in a vast ocean without any barriers. Look at yourself. Panorama!'

President Branson shouted the last word in a loud voice and the light blue curtains opened up right away, letting in an intense ray of morning light that had previously been kept out. The scene it presented was stupendous, magnificent. From the top floor of Cedir they could observe the tops of all the Masbuild buildings where gardens and drapes shone in the sunlight. Flocks of birds hovered up in the sky and disappeared on the horizon where Andrea tried desperately to get a glimpse of the end of the city. But there was no reason to look for pleasure in something beyond the invisible barriers of Milan. The view itself evoked emotion, serenity and joy of living. Yesterday's clouds had evaporated and the clear sky opened up, immense. It was nice to see such a wonder. It was beautiful. Happiness was something immense but it seemed light years away to Andrea, lost who knows where, unreachable. The young Milanese realised that he wasn't totally right.

'Freedom…' muttered Andrea.

He could barely find any truth in that word which had given him so much hope but had also taken the smile off his face. Nothing. Nothing explained the essence of things. Nothing made him feel powerful within those four walls. The wind blew against the large windows making them quaver and the young Milanese began the slow descent toward resignation.

'But can't you see how beautiful universal happiness is?' exclaimed Branson getting up from the chair and moving to look out of the window. 'Let's keep this lack of freedom because at least it means we have peace. You don't know how the ancients would envy you?'

He paused. He saw a plane flash past in the clear sky.

'In the times of nations' continued Branson. 'There was something called "politics", an archaic method to regulate the relations between citizens and the institutions to achieve collective well-being. It was based on a parliamentary debate but gradually it degenerated into a deal between just a few, between the rich and the poor, the intelligent and the unintelligent. For example, they voted in favour of the masses and at the same time they were despised. In the meantime the great innovations at the end of the twentieth century imposed an effort to foresee the capability to change the world and its men. Especially the Internet, which didn't give a precise social entity and in a certain sense it virtually put the distinction between classes to one side. Insignificant individuals could become protagonists with a simple "click" on the computer. They could intervene in business or any decision-making and almost in the consciences of men of power. Many asked themselves what the future of politics would be. At that time democracy was adopted as the mainstream form of government and there was a fear of losing it, given that it was considered the absolutely best system. However, there wasn't the risk of an oppressive elite with immense power because by then millions of people had their own computer and Internet and they would have been able to run over an arrogant and corrupt political class as easily as a good managerial class. When politics became everybody's business, the principal of representation collapsed: politics ended up being everywhere and nowhere; when the masses started to own it, it fatally coincided with the de-politicisation of the world. When the Revolutions broke out, the world had already adopted liberalism for decades. And in a short time it had degenerated into anarchy-liberalism, an infinitesimal contrast among nations and individuals. Chaos exploded like a chain reaction involving and destroying everything year after year. Sooner or later there would have been a total collapse but blood continued to be shed and after the fifth revolt in Seattle people no longer had the will to fight and preferred to call a cease fire and be happy ever after...'

Andrea thought about the old man and how tired he was of fighting and how he had insisted on keeping the eyes on the world far away from him. He thought about it quickly so as not to lose track of the discussion with President Branson.

'…The Global Corp. foundation proposed to re-establish order, but the new order wasn't going to be the version handed down from the old one. First of all, someone had to take the reins of the situation and guide everyone in one direction. This decisive step was made by Congress, a fundamental element of the Global Corp. *technopolis*. It was a managerial group made up of ten *venture capitalists* covering the same number of world continents. The boss of Congress is me and in fact it is myself who chooses the members every six months. They are techno-brains, highly talented people who have transformed the old and languid regulations into a technocracy, or better still, a totalitarian and benign biocracy which imitates everything to its own image and likeness. Everyone is equal everyone has the same interests but the thought of Global Corp. is always the same, omnipresent in every one of them. We have been able to repress, or rather, moderate freedom of speech within the individual himself; we have been able to avoid the individual becoming more important than Global Corp. so they can't destroy the sense of brotherhood within the community. The net already nurtures a sense of brotherhood; it was once used by the revolutionaries to keep their "chief-less" organisation alive, then it became the suitable instrument to put different worlds all on the same plain, the global one.

'How is the happiness you promise possible?' Andrea's mind was fixed on that snatched smile.

He looked down through the large window but he couldn't see the road below. He tried to justify in every possible way his incapacity to act.

'Well, the question of happiness is to do things in such a way that people love their subservience to Global Corp. Without economic security love for subservience can't exist. As you well know, wealth and poverty depend on political and educational causes and they are solved with multi-dimensional remedies. Collective progress expands this way: they offer new occasions of abundance to the multitudes and suppress, at least in part, old privileges. This is positive for the majority and for the overall promotion of society. A long time ago in this situation, the wealthy classes would have become bitter, they would have felt dispossessed. But me, I'm the top boss of Global Corp. and I feel proud of our new wellbeing which finally blesses the whole world. Our system follows a model driven by and founded on the client's requests, but we do things in a way that clients request only and exclusively a determined number of models that will bring happiness. By controlling people's desires we could create a levelling society, based on a necessary minimum, but we don't do that because progress is judged more plausible with a further enrichment of opulence than with a reduction of privation. People would notice easily if they lived in bad conditions. At the same time, we need to maintain a limited and self-sufficient well-being, eradicating some assets that are cumbersome, dangerous and inconsistent with what Global Corp. expects. At this point everyone can have everything and everyone can have the same things without there being a war among the greedy. We all walk together toward progress and no-one remains behind. This is the miracle at Global Corp.

The economy exploits this condition to the best. In the old systems, the principal of competition had led to the bankruptcy of many companies while the successful ones devoured every resource right down to the last drop, according to their own interests. Fair companies have never existed. Therefore Global Corp. thought it necessary to put a centralised and global economy in place, aiming at improving society and not just personal pleasures. Linking up every aspect of doing business to the global uniformity of the Net, Global Corp. has become a centralised organism and it has been the right choice for creating a united society. Global Corp. needs precise and punctual data in order to run the economy efficiently. To talk about Congress and Compagnia is the same thing. It's stupid to create separate organisms. It all depends on the cost of operations; two organisms mean twice the expenses compared to having just one bigger entity. One large organism can carry out operations that save time and keep them busy all the time: small ones go through cycles of inactivity. Firms in competition with each other have to multiply their efforts; centralization instead, is always efficient. Centralised organisms can accumulate and process information more efficiently than individual and widespread business men can. The image of the computer makes the idea clearer: it's absurd to solve complicated equations on lots of tiny calculators since just one electronic brain can carry out trillions and trillions of operations in a second. Therefore, Global Corp. isn't competition, but planning. Competition in itself wastes environmental and energy resources; centralised planning instead works, it saves energy and guarantees a direct and safe control.'

'The Darkening, is that energy saving?'

'Not only. The energy crisis is now a closed case. It's been twenty years since we discovered fusion power and we built numerous solar plants in the Sahara. However, we of Global Corp. are reluctant to use total illumination. Such an action could lead to the dispersion of the city centre or the heart of Global Corp. In this regard we decided to adopt the trick of the Men of the Night.'

'You make use of fear, don't you?'

'It isn't fear. It's just a self-limiting rule which starts at eight o'clock every evening until seven in the morning. It doesn't alter the peace of the community in any way, nor the trust in Global Corp. Maybe one day, when illumination isn't considered destabilising, all these tricks will not be useful anymore and like magic the Days of Light will suddenly increase but it is still to be seen. Everything has to serve and guarantee centralisation.'

'Let's suppose information is better if run locally, that centralization overloads the organizers with too much data. Let's suppose that an individual organizer who is familiar with the problems he has to face every day, makes better decisions than the global organizers. Let's suppose that competition works in the way old economists had conceived it, that monopoly is not at all better than private...'

'Everything you've said has passed, Mr. Rossi. Satellite technology now enables us to reach every corner of the earth in just a few seconds; the Net enables us to channel the economy into one flow, the same world population is centralised in cities. The old system is extinct. Local governments no longer exist, provincialism doesn't exist either. The world is all equal, from Mexico City to Peking, from London to Cape Town.'

'But how can you say old systems aren't any good?'

'Well, you can't do experiments with the economy but you can see what has happened in the past. Without doubt the old systems were a step ahead but they didn't work forever. The subdivision of classes, the ignored poor, the looted environment, everyone forced to live under the constant barrage of commercial blandishment. Unacceptable. The new system is globalisation. Globalisation is the system of a compact and solid economy. Its indefinite and gradual development has never foreseen catastrophic crises, although there have been people like the revolutionaries who were contrary to all of this. The term "globalisation" in fact suggests a futuristic vision of vast and relentless economic processes that went ahead all over the world, treading on forests, monuments and traditions without keeping the weak individuals in mind. Globalisation, right or wrong, seemed unstoppable. And this is where we have ended up. Naturally in time many old traditions and habits have got lost on the way, lost in the name of progress, but at the end, Global Corp. has not betrayed the trust of its people. It has given them a home, a job, money, entertainment, well-being…'

'…and you have forced them to live a dream with a happy ending!'

'No dreams Mr. Rossi. This is reality. On the contrary, God is a dream and History is a nightmare we try to wake up from.'

He paused and went back to his desk.

'You need to know that fantasy isn't educative.' said Branson once he sat down. 'Man who looks within himself and doesn't take care of the external world around him must be nailed to reality. A withdrawn life and contemplative activity aren't materially useful to society. The Compagnia leans on supporting pillars who must be active, lively and functional; there isn't time to ask oneself the reason for things, the whys, if that means preventing the advance of progress. We need to go ahead all together since the worst sin against our fellowmen isn't hate but misanthropic indifference: this is the essence of inhumanity. I repeat, ours isn't a society founded on individual egoism. Everything is connected to the motto "Community, Identity, Stability". Controlling the genes of every human being, Global Corp. has finally got divine power and can't find a limit or an impediment in its action. Man is limited for reasons of security. Man must no longer be like a virus that spreads and destroys every form of life. Biocentrism has definitely ousted anthropocentrism and has given new hope of survival from degradation and catastrophe to humanity. Long Live Global Corp!'

'It's horrible!' Andrea answered back indignant.

'Ah! Morality!' exclaimed Branson in a sardonic tone. 'Morality is the last bastion of a coward. If I do not error, it was the first obstacle to be faced when genetic engineering obtained its first success. And well, anyway, every historical age has had its dark sides. The Industrial Era of the nineteenth century had brought pollution, the Information Age brought about the problem of privacy and the bio economy the problem of ethics. However to be noted are the great steps we have made and the results we have achieved. Cloning, transgenic food, eugenics, they have given us the chance to know more about the life of man and how to make it perfect.'

With the word 'perfect' silence fell over the room. Andrea didn't reply. He felt so imperfect in that precise moment. His thoughts no longer followed a logical order, they were all jumbled up and had taken on a form without rhyme or reason. Andrea looked out of the window for a last time. The golden reflection on the window hit his eyes and blinded him for a moment concealing the view. For a moment he didn't see the gardens or the drapes, the blue sky, the flock of birds fly. He only saw an inner darkness and turned back with his eyes closed, maybe for the pain to his eyes or perhaps for fear of seeing himself. He moved away from the window, and keeping his back to the President of Global Corp., moved to the middle of the room away from the light, from Masbuild buildings, from super fast planes and cheerful melodies. He refused all of this. This could make him feel worse but he obstinately refused it all. He couldn't bear the idea of having to live in a welcoming world, aware of its falseness. He didn't have the courage to look into people's eyes and see the in justices they endured. For Andrea refusing all was the right thing to do.

'I can't accept this.' Andrea said suddenly in a husky dry voice.

'Don't be stupid, Mr. Rossi.' warned Branson from his desk. 'If you hate the place where you are, you end up losing everything and there's no turning back. Believe me, once you've lost something you want it back desperately. That's what happens. You're still in time to change your way and catch up with us. Your memory will be cancelled all in one go, radical changes will be made and you'll be able to be re-born, start again from scratch and forget all of this. This type of experiment is rare but it has been done once or twice with success. Just yesterday a natural son asked to be re-programmed, not being able to bear the memory of the past. It was a certain Marco Gandolfi.'

Andrea went stiff. Marco. His friend. The only person remaining in this world. He too had gone out of his life.

'Listen to me, Mr. Rossi.' continued Branson without noticing how the young Milanese had turned to stone. 'Happiness is not lost. You only have to go to the Celera Genomics laboratories and everything will vanish into oblivion. What have you got to lose?'

Andrea had lost his parents, friends, hope, everything. What had he got left? Global Corp. and its promises. No, he would never shake hands with his enemy. All that happiness would never have given him back trust in himself. What for anyway? To become a vegetable incapable of understanding and wanting by himself. No. His answer was 'no'.

'I don't want to be a monster estranged from myself.' contradicted Andrea turning to face the President of Global Corp.

'You were the one who killed, Mr. Rossi!' accused Branson pointing his finger at him. 'You are the monster...!'

Andrea felt his heart tighten and contract with pain. This is where the blow was inflicted. Another dart shot and stuck into his sensitive, weak and fragile flesh. Stop! It was unbearable!

'And you've become an individual who thinks for himself and is suspicious toward those who are around you so much so that you're not friends with anyone.'

Stop! Andrea repeated this word to himself ad nauseam. Laura's tears, Alberoni's worried face, the melancholic expression of Marco, the astonished eyes of the witnesses during the shooting, they all came back to him and all of a sudden he felt ashamed for what he had done. He had neglected the others, he had kept them distant. He was a poor egoist. This was his sin and he couldn't escape it. Change lifestyle? Useless, because that wasn't the right way to atonement. Andrea's answer remained 'no'.

'Mr. Branson, I refuse your offer.' said Andrea in a loud voice looking at his fate in the face. 'What will happen to me now?'

'Your individual instinct isn't acceptable.' answered Branson pressing a button.

The *dvd-screen* changed image passing from the title 'Universal Genetic Archives' to an infra-red film. In the greyish darkness he could clearly see the figure of a man destroying the central mains unit with his shoulders in his own room. The time at the bottom right hand corner of the screen said three in the morning. Andrea recognised himself and felt even more ashamed. He was the guilty one. He was the monster.

'I advise you to think again about your choices.' said Branson turning off the big screen with a clap of his hands.

'Otherwise I'll be eliminated?' asked Andrea.

'If one is different, he must be isolated. Or eliminated, as you say. It's better for one person to suffer, rather than having everybody corrupted by your individualistic manias. Non-orthodoxy doesn't threaten the life of one miserable individual, rather it hits the foundations of society itself. The murderer kills only the individual. After all what is an individual? A microscopic cell in the body of society. But we aren't a dictatorship and we don't deprive people of their lives. You are free to choose, you're free to go, if you want, as long as you save us the inconvenience!'

'But I want inconvenience!'

'We don't want it. We prefer to live in comfort and peace.'

'But I don't want comfort and peace! I want God, I want poetry, I want real danger, I want madness, I want freedom!'

'Mr. Rossi, you're asking for the right to be unhappy!'

'Well, ok then! I'm asking for the right to be unhappy!'

'Without mentioning the right to become old, ugly and impotent; the right to have syphilis and cancer; the right to have little to eat, the right to be despicable; the right to live I'

Andrea stood still on hearing those sad words President Branson had said to him. This was the road to be taken through and through. And now the wisest thing to do was leave that place and go back to breathing the autumn air. He needed a good breath of fresh air.

'I accept all this.' Andrea finally said.

'Alright Mr. Rossi. There's the door.'

The President of Global Corp. made no comment about Andrea's decision and he started tidying the books in his safe as well as the diary. Andrea didn't ask to have it back. He will leave it with "The Divine Comedy",

"Romeo and Juliet" and the other book. That was the only satisfaction. He turned, resigned, and slowly he went toward the lift. Once inside it he could see the President of Global Corp. stare at him from his desk and say something to him.

'*Memento postridie*! Remember tomorrow!'

Mr. Branson's phrase sounded very familiar. It was the same phrase the old man had used, said with the same solemnity. There was no difference between the two versions. They were both two types of honey with the same convincing taste. The lift doors closed before Andrea had the chance to respond and he began his descent to the ground floor. Memento postridie. Andrea thought again about that expression and in the meantime he had got lost again, ending up in a limbo from where there was no escape.

X

All the questions had been asked, all the answers had been given. There was nothing else. Only the world as it had been conceived by Global Corp. And here were the lines of people who were going in and out of the automatic doors, satisfied with their short work day, happy never to have felt so good thinking about their day plans. Andrea left the Fichampon with the flow of people coming out into the inner square. He stopped after about walking two metres while tens of people passed by touching his shoulders, but he didn't react nor did he move out of the way. He was absent, empty, arid with a continuous striving inside to understand the complexity of his life. When you clean up your life to start a new one, what are you left with? Answer: a white space. Alternative answer: freedom. Life without ties nor duties that you've always desired. But when you compare yourself to that freedom, to that white space, you feel nothing but fear. Because freedom is like staring at a shapeless emptiness, a realm without structure, without roots, like a stone that rolls downhill and falling into the sea drowns in its mediocrity. Andrea had this presentiment, hidden behind that big word 'freedom', and it made him afraid but he truly knew that it was a real freedom. The life without duties promised by Global Corp. wasn't at all free or spontaneous; on the contrary, it was an inseparable tie imposed by the mother society on him. Global Corp. had saved the fate of the world from chaos and so it thought it had the right to dominate people's lives. But how could he help people free themselves from that chain? Andrea had helped himself and he had failed with Marco. Did he have a chance with the remaining four million nine hundred and ninety-nine thousand, nine hundred and ninety nine habitants in Milan? He was losing from the start because no-one would have given up that delicate umbilical cord which fed them and made them addicted to it. Besides, Andrea's situation was precarious. How should he have behaved toward the others knowing now that behind everything there was an astute intrigue, concealing the truth? How could he move tranquilly now knowing that every one of his moves was surveyed, that in every road he would have felt the breath of Global Corp. down his neck? Andrea looked up and saw the top floor of Cedir. Then he looked at the sky and remembered that his every step corresponded to a 'beep' of the satellite system. He knew. He knew. He knew too much.

Andrea started walking again and got on the first *transports* that came by the bus stop. In the middle of the crowd no-one seemed to take any notice of him. No-one gave him looks of reproach, no-one pointed at him behind his back whispering to their colleagues 'that's the man who killed those poor people'. Nothing. Total indifference. And Andrea suffered knowing that the indifference was the result of his indifference which had taken him out of the world, leaving him alone against everyone. He suddenly got the idea to run away. Run far, far away. He could run to one of the many stations and catch the first Monorail SV to Malpensa without telling anyone. In an hour he would be at the airport and surely he would have found a flight departing for the other side of the world. And then? To go as far as Los Angeles or as far as Sydney didn't change things very much. There he would have found a square with other four *iperco-ops*, a Fichampon, a Cedir, an area for the Public Gardens. The climate, the geographic position changed, but lifestyle was the same. The world unfortunately was all the same. And even worse, the whole surface of the earth was dominated by satellites. There was no escape. The President of Global Corp. would have persecuted him as far away as necessary to keep an eye on him. There was no escape.

The *transport* slowed down and then quickened again as it went past Piazza Duomo. Andrea thought of another alternative. He could throw himself off the Monorail in motion and land in the unspoilt countryside among the ruins of the old world far from any possible bio-agricultural establishments. And then? What would he have found waiting for him? The Commies maybe. Or maybe a pile of skeletons gnawed by fierce beasts. At the end he would have been even more alone, in a panic, forced to refuse well-being and forced to live in the mud. There was nothing to do. Escaping from Milan like this didn't have much chance of being successful. Nor did hiding in the old man's shelter seem a good idea. Living surrounded by the dust of old books wasn't the maximum of his aspirations either and moreover he couldn't risk getting noticed and let this hidden treasure end up in the wrong hands, that is Global Corp.'s. Hiding, therefore, was out of discussion. What other choices remained? He could go to a *gerial* and live with old people, maybe with Marco's parents, and continue his discourses with the old man that he had left unfinished. Yes, that could be a good experience. On one side, wisdom and the past, on the other, well-being and serenity. The only problem was there would always be the restraint by Global Corp. They wouldn't have let him stay in a *gerial*, and even if he had tried to get there, they would have found him very easily.

The only option left was to cancel his memory but Andrea was reluctant to do this. He was in absolute disagreement with the only offer made by the President of Global Corp. There must have been another choice, another way to solve the matter- a more human way than an artificial machine that cancelled any guilt as if they were chocolate stains. Andrea forced himself to think. The transport stopped suddenly and the young Milanese, looking out of the window, realised he had reached his destination.

Room 221b in the apartment Belfiore was in the dark and even if there was some afternoon sun there were no great changes. Andrea entered, dragging his feet. The sitting room and bedroom were just as he had left it, just like the kitchen and bathroom. The central mains unit was still there, all smashed up. Global Corp. out of spite, hadn't even bothered to fix it. Andrea gazed around and sat down at his desk, his computer on one side and the *dvd-screen* on the other. There were some people who had the two devices all in one, but Andrea had other things on his mind. For now, all he wanted to do was write, let off steam, doodle and get his mind working. He opened the desk drawer and saw the empty space where he had kept the red diary. Goodbye writing, thought Andrea. Anyway, whoever had come to take his dairy away, had left his pen there at the back of the drawer. Andrea picked it up not caring if there was a possible video camera hidden somewhere. He held it firmly between his index finger and thumb, in full view, then he stared at the bare white wall. Moved by his instinct, that criminal, abnormal instinct, source of his every pain and truth, he began writing on the wall in a somewhat messy style of hand writing. Words came out on their own accord as usual, only this time Andrea was fully aware of what he was writing.

Letter V – Milan 14th November 2073

To those who will come after me. To when Global Corp will be too old to support its past .To the future, a soul in pain writes his last words.

Global Corp. has launched me an ultimatum. I have never lost faith in myself, in my thoughts or memories, in human things and I will not be duped by the astuteness of the technocrats. My conscience isn't asleep, it will remain awake until the sunset of my existence and beyond. I am the original copy of man and as such I will look reality in the face, its finiteness, its transience. I am only a man of flesh and bones who in thirty years' time will turn to dust but I am convinced that within us there is a strength capable of lasting forever. The sun rises, the stars align the seasons go round, they are all signs of this spiritual force. The secret of life lies in it and not in our genetic code. I don't care what others think, they know what I have discovered beyond the senses. In my dreams I have seen another world, I have felt other sensations. Sublime.

I, however, am here and who knows where that world lies. This is how things stand. But I am free because I have chosen to be so, because I know what I want to do. Nothing and no-one will be able to suppress MY own decision. I have followed MY way and I have reached MY goal. Someone may find it ambiguous, someone may consider it pointless, but as I have just said I don't care. I have found true happiness in a parallel world to this one, beyond time and space. After only a week, memories have gone, lost, but a place exists where I can recover them and re-live the emotions of before. I want to end it all with this world! I want to touch true eternity with my finger! I only hope that my action reaches the highest summits...

The text covered most of the wall. Andrea re-read it a few times, feeling fulfilled, by what he had written. Meanwhile, he gradually decided on a good plan to escape from that hostile world. The conversations and reflections of a few hours ago no longer had any importance. Once he had finished reading, he let his pen drop to the floor and went over to the central mains unit. He opened a space between the remains of the smashed up circuit and, with a strong yank, he pulled at the long bundle of cables. It was very long. He went back to his desk, and without stopping or reflecting, without indulging much, he carried on with his task. He pulled the chair out from below the desk and put it under one of the neon lights, then he took out the ceiling light bulb so he could see the hook that had been holding it. He finally took the bundle of cables after he had tied one end to the hook and made a nice noose, just wide enough for his head to enter. He put it around his neck with decision, without any fear and got up onto the chair. From up there, he gave a last look at his room that in life he had never really appreciated much. The lights were switched off, the various clocks were still, every form of technology was dead. Andrea looked straight ahead and with a kick, he knocked the chair away from beneath his feet. The yank broke his neck instantly. There was no suffocated shout, only silence. Silence. Silence. Finally silence.

All his worries and uneasiness slipped away. Eternal sleep was the only place where Global Corp. couldn't reach him. And so Andrea died, crushed by the relentless wheels of History.

October 2000 – June 2001